LAYING IT ON THE LINE

Just because the game clock has stopped, don't believe for a single second that the hearts of ten basketball players on the court have quit pounding.

It's not possible.

That same intense rhythm beats inside the chests of the players and coaches on the sidelines for the Michigan State Spartans and the Trojans of Troy University.

Only 6.9 seconds remain in regulation time, with underdog Troy leading 64–62.

The Spartans' eighteen-year-old freshman point guard sensation Malcolm McBride glares into the eyes of his defender, Roko Bacic, with Malcolm clad in green and Roko in cardinal red.

"Don't even think you can stop me from scoring," says Malcolm. "This is the real world we're living in, not a damn storybook."

"If I don't stop you, maybe you'll trip over your big mouth," says Roko, whose teammates call him "Red Bull" for his mop of curly red hair and boundless energy.

Malcolm has earned a tag, too—"One and Done."

But it's not something anyone really calls him to his face.

The media gave him that name during his senior year in high school, when Malcolm declared he'd enter the NBA draft as soon as he was eligible—after one year of college ball.

BOOKS BY PAUL VOLPONI

THE FINAL FOUR

THE FINAL FOUR

PAUL VOLPONI

speak
An Imprint of Penguin Group (USA) Inc.

SPEAK

Published by the Penguin Group

Penguin Group (USA) Inc., 345 Hudson Street, New York, New York 10014, U.S.A.

Penguin Group (Canada), 90 Eglinton Avenue East, Suite 700, Toronto, Ontario, Canada M4P 2Y3

(a division of Pearson Penguin Canada Inc.)

Penguin Books Ltd, 80 Strand, London WC2R 0RL, England

Penguin Ireland, 25 St Stephen's Green, Dublin 2, Ireland (a division of Penguin Books Ltd)

Penguin Group (Australia), 250 Camberwell Road, Camberwell, Victoria 3124, Australia

(a division of Pearson Australia Group Pty Ltd)

Penguin Books India Pvt Ltd, 11 Community Centre, Panchsheel Park, New Delhi – 110 017, India

Penguin Group (NZ), 67 Apollo Drive, Rosedale, Auckland 0632, New Zealand

(a division of Pearson New Zealand Ltd.)

Penguin Books (South Africa) (Pty) Ltd, 24 Sturdee Avenue, Rosebank, Johannesburg 2196, South Africa

Penguin Books Ltd, Registered Offices: 80 Strand, London WC2R 0RL, England

First published in the United States of America by Viking, a member of Penguin Group (USA) Inc., 2012
Published by Speak, an imprint of Penguin Group (USA) Inc., 2013

15 17 19 20 18 16 14

THE LIBRARY OF CONGRESS HAS CATALOGED THE VIKING EDITION AS FOLLOWS:

Volponi, Paul.

The Final Four / by Paul Volponi.

p. cm.

Summary: Four players at the Final Four of the NCAA basketball tournament struggle with the
pressures of tournament play and the expectations of society at large.

ISBN: 978-0-670-01264-0 (hardcover)

[1. Basketball—Fiction. 2. NCAA Basketball Tournament—Fiction. 3. Conduct of life—Fiction.
4. African Americans—Fiction.] I. Title.

PZ7.V8877Fi 2012

[Fic]—dc23

2011011587

Speak ISBN 978-0-14-242385-1

Printed in the United States of America
Set in Granjon

This text is dedicated to the lifeblood of college basketball: the players,
who are all too often viewed as the product instead of the source.

Special Thanks:

Joy Peskin

Regina Hayes

Don Weisberg

Rosemary Stimola

Leila Sales

Abigail Powers

David Cipollone

Senad Ahmetovic

April Volponi

Sabrina Volponi

Jim Cocoros

THE FINAL FOUR

"I am sure that no man can derive more pleasure from money or power than I do from seeing a pair of basketball goals in some out of the way place."

—James Naismith, who invented the game of basketball in Springfield, Massachusetts, in 1891

SATURDAY, MARCH 31, 7:13 P.M. (CT)
THE LOUISIANA SUPERDOME

J ust because the game clock has stopped, don't believe for a single second that the hearts of the ten basketball players on the court have quit pounding.

It's not possible.

That same intense rhythm beats inside the chests of the players and coaches on the sidelines for the Michigan State Spartans and the Trojans of Troy University.

Only 6.9 seconds remain in regulation time, with underdog Troy leading 64–62.

The Spartans' eighteen-year-old freshman point guard sensation Malcolm McBride glares into the eyes of his defender,

Roko Bacic, with Malcolm clad in green and Roko in cardinal red.

"Don't even think you can stop me from scoring," says Malcolm. "This is the real world we're living in, not a damn storybook."

Then Malcolm kisses the fingers on his left hand, before touching them to the tattooed portrait on his right arm. The name TRISHA is arched above her carefully detailed face indelibly inked into Malcolm's black skin.

"If I don't stop you, maybe you'll trip over your big mouth," says Roko, whose teammates call him "Red Bull" for his mop of curly red hair and boundless energy.

Malcolm has earned a tag, too—"One and Done."

But it's not something anyone really calls him to his face.

The media gave him that name during his senior year in high school, when Malcolm declared he'd enter the NBA draft as soon as he was eligible—after one year of college ball.

As a stripe-shirted referee hands the basketball to a player with the word STATE across his chest, Malcolm and Roko begin their fight for position.

Drenched in sweat, their arms and legs slide off of one another's—grappling, pushing, and pulling to the limits the refs will allow.

The Spartans have only until the count of five to inbound the ball. And as the referee's hand slices the air for the fourth time, Malcolm finally shakes free.

He receives the inbounds pass, restarting the game clock.

In a millisecond, Malcolm sizes up Red Bull, who defends him tightly, denying the opportunity for a deep three-point basket to win.

So Malcolm makes his move to the hoop. First, he stutter-steps, disrupting Roko's balance. Then he explodes to his right, before cutting the angle sharply left.

With little more than a second remaining, Malcolm stops his dribble on a dime, driving his legs into the slatted wooden floor.

Then Malcolm's wiry six-foot-three-inch frame takes air.

Red Bull shadows him all the way, just a fraction behind.

At the height of his leap, Malcolm focuses his sight on the rim as Red Bull's outstretched hands flash across his face.

Despite the strain in his muscles, Malcolm's touch is light. And he releases the rock like a feather onto a breeze.

Neither Malcolm nor Red Bull sees the shot go in as their bodies tumble to the court. But they both hear the clean *swish* of the ball through the netting before the Louisiana Superdome explodes in sound, and the clock is reset for overtime.

From that morning's national newspaper:

CINDERELLA CRASHES
FINAL FOUR BALL

NEW ORLEANS, La. — Yes, Cinderella has arrived at the Big Dance in the Big Easy. The Trojans of

Troy University—the Cinderella story of the Men's NCAA Basketball Tournament—will take on the heavily favored Michigan State Spartans in the first semifinal at the Final Four, tonight at 5:07 p.m. (CT). The nearly 56,000 fans expected to fill the Louisiana Superdome will represent the largest crowd for which the Trojans, whose home arena seats a mere 4,000, have ever played.

"March Madness" is what the NCAA Tournament is called, and for good reason. Few pundits could have predicted that Troy, which had never won an NCAA Tournament game before, would still be dancing in this single-elimination tournament that has so far sent more than 60 teams packing over nearly three weeks of competition. In comparison, Michigan State, a perennial contender for the title, has been crowned National Champion twice and reached the Final Four on several other occasions.

Controversial freshman and soon to be NBA draft–bound Malcolm McBride, who made national headlines yesterday by criticizing the NCAA and stating that the players putting on this tournament should receive part of the over $700 million generated by it, is the Spartans' leading scorer and top trash-talker.

"This isn't even going to be a game. It's going

to be more like a workout on national TV," said McBride, who hails from the tough Brewster-Douglass Housing Projects on the East Side of Detroit. "The clock's going to strike midnight early for these Cinderella Troy boys. The glass slipper doesn't fit. They're going home as pumpkins. And I'll tell them that on the court to their faces, too."

Junior Roko Bacic is the Trojans' high-energy leader. Born and raised in the war-torn and rebuilding country of Croatia along the coast of Eastern Europe, Bacic has experienced his share of intense battles as well. Bacic figures to guard McBride one-on-one most of the night. How will he respond to the brash freshman's trash talking?

"He has freedom of speech. That's very special. It's one of the things I love most about the U.S.," said Bacic. "But I also find [McBride] to be pretty annoying. He can say whatever he wants. Now he just has to back it up on the basketball court, or look very foolish."

An American film and music buff, the redheaded Croatian credits his study of entertainment with helping him to better learn the English language and its accents.

"Even if McBride scores a big basket or two," said Bacic, before slipping into his best Arnold

Schwarzenegger voice from *The Terminator*, "on defense, *I'll be back*."

The last time the Spartans and Trojans met for stakes this high was in the Trojan War of Greek mythology, when the Spartans left a huge wooden horse outside the gates of Troy. Believing the gift to be a sign that the war was over, the Trojans brought the horse into their city. That night, the Spartan soldiers who had hidden inside the horse opened the gates of Troy so their army could burn the city down.

Earlier this week, Troy coach Alvin Kennedy showed his players Hollywood's version of that mythical war in the movie *Troy*.

"My team loved it," said Kennedy. "They'll be sure not to fall for any trick plays now. They even liked the fact that the Spartans won in the movie, because together as a team, we're ready to rewrite history."

In the nightcap at 7:47 (CT), the North Carolina Tar Heels and Duke Blue Devils, a pair of traditional blue bloods with nine National Championships and over 30 Final Four appearances between them, will compete for the right to take on the Troy/Michigan State winner in the championship game on Monday night.

Troy University Trojans—Troy, Alabama

No.	Name	Pos.	Ht.	Wt.	Yr.	Hometown
23	Bacic, Roko	G	6-4	205	Jr.	Zagreb, Croatia
13	Boyce, Aaron	F	6-6	218	Sr.	New Orleans, La.
45	Rice, Crispin	C	6-10	238	Sr.	Vinemont, Ala.
32	Hall, Tom	G	6-1	190	Sr.	Olive Hill, Ky.
30	Delaney, Clay	F	6-8	225	So.	Anniston, Ala.

Coach: Alvin Kennedy (5th year)

Team Colors: cardinal red, black and silver

Mascot: T-Roy (Trojan soldier)

Summary: Surprise winners of nine straight games, team chemistry is the Trojans' strong suit. Coach Alvin Kennedy has his players believing in themselves and not acting like tourists at the Final Four. For the Trojans to win, Roko "Red Bull" Bacic, an emerging pro prospect, must find a way to contain All-American Malcolm McBride. Undersized center Crispin Rice must stay out of foul trouble against Michigan State's enormous frontcourt. Sweet-shooting Aaron Boyce, a New Orleans native, must show the same resolve that helped him outlast Hurricane Katrina in the Superdome when he faces the defensive-minded Spartans.

Michigan State Spartans—East Lansing, Michigan

No.	Name	Pos.	Ht.	Wt.	Yr.	Hometown
11	McBride, Malcolm	G	6-3	195	Fr.	Detroit, Mich.
5	Wilkins, DeJuan	F	6-9	260	Jr.	Euclid, Ohio
25	Cousins, John	C	7-0	270	Sr.	Flint, Mich.
14	Pitt, William	G	6-4	212	Sr.	Springfield, Mo.
15	Serling, Ed	F	6-7	200	Sr.	Willoughby, Ohio

Coach: Eddie Barker (14th year)

Team Colors: green and white

Mascot: Sparty (Spartan soldier)

Summary: The Spartans have been here before—the Trojans have not—and succeeded under coach Eddie Barker. If Barker can control the shot selection and attitude of freshman point guard Malcolm McBride, a sure lottery pick in June's NBA draft, the Spartans should cruise here. "Grizzly Bear" Cousins and "Baby Bear" Wilkins are no Yogi and Boo-Boo, and should devour rebounds against the smaller Trojans. The Michigan State bench is considerably stronger as well, even in name, boasting a junior reserve named Michael Jordan. Even Sparty, the foam-rubber-costumed mascot, is taller and more buff than the Trojans' T-Roy.

7:15 P.M. (CT)
ON A CABLE SPORTS NETWORK PROVIDING
LIVE UPDATES FROM THE FINAL FOUR

Announcer: Welcome back to *Sports News 'Round the Clock*. Tonight we are truly all things Final Four. Just moments ago, Michigan State freshman Malcolm McBride, who all year has declared himself to be "one and done" as he awaits entry into the NBA, buried a clutch shot at the buzzer, sending the first semifinal game at the Final Four into overtime. The dramatic basket kept the Spartans' hopes for another national title alive and put another inconceivable celebration by the underdog Trojans of Troy on hold.

It has seemingly been all about Malcolm McBride for the past thirty-two hours or so. Now, in case you missed it, here are selected highlights of yesterday's question-and-answer session with the media and a trio of Michigan State players. Nearly all of the questions, of course, are aimed at the outspoken McBride. His lightning-rod responses have since drawn a thunderstorm of criticism from defenders of the current college basketball system and a swift counterstatement by his school. And that thunderstorm continues to reverberate tonight as he leads the Spartans into overtime in the Superdome.

On screen, Malcolm McBride sits between two of his teammates, John "Grizzly Bear" Cousins and DeJuan "Baby Bear" Wilkins, at a long table on a raised platform. Each player has a microphone set before him and a folded piece of cardboard displaying his name. The young men are framed by the backdrop of a blue curtain embossed with NCAA *in large white lettering.*

Reporter: Malcolm, you've previously stated that you only chose college because of the NBA's current rule of not allowing players to enter the league until a year after their high school class graduates. As I recall, you even referred to it once as "being held hostage." But now that you've spent a season at Michigan State, have you grown from the college experience? And will you be back next year, or will this truly be a "one and done" situation for you?

Malcolm: I basically came here a grown man, with all I'd seen and been through. No school is going to teach me more than that. I guess a year out of the projects helped to keep me alive. But my parents still live there. So my plan is to go pro as quick as I can, enter the NBA draft, and cash that fat paycheck for me and my family.

Second Reporter: Mr. McBride, when people hear you talk about the money, should they be turned off? I suppose what I'm really asking is, do you have any respect for the term "student athlete," or are you and other "one and done" players just using the college system to eventually line your own pockets?

Malcolm: To tell you the truth, I think the system is using *me* to make money. I play here for free. I don't get a nickel. My parents even had to pay for their own hotel room in New Orleans. And there's always some NCAA investigator wanting to make sure that anybody looking to become my agent didn't slip them fifty bucks for gas money to drive here. But I heard that the NCAA makes something like seven hundred million dollars on this tournament, and that my school could make fifteen mil. I know part of that number's off my back, my sweat. That's like slavery. I could blow out my knee on any play and lose my career. Then I'd be left with nothing.

Malcolm's teammates on either side of him are looking at each other now, nervously shifting around in their seats.

Second Reporter: You don't think that free tuition and board at a major college is worth something?

Malcolm: No, it's not. That's like McDonald's giving you a free hamburger because you work there. Big deal. They had the patties, buns, and pickles ready to sell anyway. The professors and the school buildings are already there, right? What does it cost them to add one more student into the mix—nothing? But how much money do I bring in? At least at Mickey D's they pay you minimum wage. Here, they lean on that student athlete stuff to stiff you, and keep you poor. They want you hungry, so you'll play harder and put on a better show. They use the NBA as your Kids Meal toy to get you in the front door.

Third Reporter: I'd like to hear something from Malcolm's team-mates. John, how do you feel about competing for your school under the current system?

John (Grizzly Bear): *(Tapping the microphone before he speaks)* I'm proud to do it, to compete as a Spartan. I don't even go to McDon-ald's anymore *(with a small laugh)*, not since I was a little kid.

Third Reporter: And DeJuan, what about you?

DeJuan (Baby Bear): I'm just following my dream: to play college ball at a high level and impress NBA scouts. That's all.

Third Reporter: So Malcolm, wouldn't everyone involved have been better off, and you less abused, if you'd spent the year play-ing professional ball overseas? You'd have gotten paid for your work there, right?

Malcolm: I don't see why I should be forced to leave my own coun-try to earn a decent living. Because I'm not nineteen yet? That's age discrimination. I can vote. I can join the U.S. army. But I can't play pro ball. Why? Because NBA owners wasted hundreds of millions on too many high school kids who couldn't cut it in the pros before? That's not me *(running his right hand back over his close-cut hair)*. Maybe I should go to work with my father in the auto plants for a year. Oh, that's right—I can't, because him and lots of other people got laid off from the assembly line. So that's two jobs I can't have.

First Reporter: Malcolm, just to follow up, obviously you've passed your first semester of classes at Michigan State, or you wouldn't be eligible to continue playing. But there have been reports that you've stopped going to class completely during your second semester, in anticipation of leaving school after the tournament concludes. If that's true, do you feel like you're manipulating the system?

Malcolm: I had to take at least six credits my first semester, and I did—passed them all. It doesn't matter if it was ballroom dancing or basketball 101. I passed. It's like the second time I took the SAT and scored so much higher. Nobody believed it. And I had to take it a third time to prove I had some natural smarts. Well, I really can't remember about this semester. It's been too much basketball and travel for my *school*. So I'll have to wait for grades in a couple of months to find out. For the second part of that question, it's like what my father always says about living in the projects, about being trapped there—no one can manipulate the system who didn't invent it, a system that was made to keep you down.

First Reporter: Malcolm, there have been whispers that you may come under NCAA investigation for receiving some type of improper benefits. Do you know anything about that?

Malcolm: All I can tell you is I've got no wheels, no watch, no rings *(looking down at his bare wrists and fingers)*, and no money in the bank. Ask anyone who knows me, anyone who sees me walking around campus. People who are jealous of me are always going to be serving up that *Haterade*. So as far as I'm concerned, those rumors come under the heading of *Child, Please*.

Third Reporter: U.S. Secretary of Education Arne Duncan has proposed that schools which don't graduate at least fifty percent of their scholarship basketball players should be banned from playing in this tournament. How do you feel about lowering your school's graduation rate by leaving early, Malcolm? What if your teammates and school pay the price for that, being banned from a future tournament?

Malcolm: I don't care about none of that. I'm looking after number one—myself. I've seen what happens in this world when you don't, when you put other people first. That's why I wear eleven on my uniform. There are two number ones in a row, to always remind me, in case I forget. I pass the rock to my teammates when they're open. That's it. Nobody can ask any more from me. And no one should.

Broadcast cuts back to the studio announcer.

Announcer: Within an hour of Malcolm McBride's comments, the Michigan State Athletics Department issued this statement *(statement appears on screen as announcer reads it)*: "We whole-heartedly believe in amateurism and the ideal of the student athlete. Our scholarship athletes abide by the rules of the NCAA and make great personal sacrifices to compete on the athletic field while maintaining their primary role as students at Michigan State." *(Cut back to announcer)* Michigan State coach Eddie Barker, who has been battling laryngitis throughout the tournament, has yet to comment.

"Where I grew up—I grew up on the north side of Akron [Ohio], lived in the projects. So those scared and lonely nights—that's every night. You hear a lot of police sirens, you hear a lot of gunfire. Things that you don't want your kids to hear growing up."

—LeBron James, who went directly from high school into the NBA

CHAPTER ONE

MALCOLM McBRIDE

7:18 P.M. (CT)

The Goodyear Blimp isn't as pumped up as Malcolm, standing inside the Michigan State huddle. If it were, it would be providing a national TV audience with a video feed from the surface of Mars right now, instead of an aerial view of the Superdome.

Coach Barker, who sports a middle-age paunch and stands almost a head shorter than Malcolm, is the focus of the Spartans' attention.

"Seize on the momentum Malcolm just gave us," Coach Barker preaches to his players in a strained and raspy voice. "That shot he made destroyed them. Believe me, they're deflated. They'll be dragging out there. They haven't got the heart or stomach for this kind of pressure. We do!"

The players standing closest to Malcolm, Grizzly Bear Cousins and Baby Bear Wilkins, each drape an arm across his shoulders.

Malcolm feels their weight as they try to lift themselves and overcome their exhaustion.

"They're tired. We're not. Stay tough on defense, but watch—" says Barker over the crowd noise, before his voice finally falters.

Malcolm raises his head from the huddle, gazing into the packed stands. Sitting nine rows behind the Michigan State bench are his parents.

His mama, a lunchroom worker in a Detroit elementary school, is cheering wildly.

Though Malcolm can't hear her over the crowd, he reads her lips mouthing, "Go, son! Go!"

Malcolm's father is much more reserved. He claps his callused hands, nodding his head beneath a cap that reads BUILT TOUGH, the motto of the car company that released him after twenty-three years on their assembly line.

Coach Barker sticks a hand out into the middle of the huddle, and his players quickly pile theirs on top.

Barker punishes his vocal cords to get out a single word: "Victory!"

In unison, the players repeat it, breaking the huddle.

Then Malcolm gives some instructions of his own.

"Grizz, I want you to knock that Red Bull dude senseless with a hard screen. I can't have him hawking me everywhere without consequences."

"Done," says Grizzly, through the growing shadow of a sandpaper beard.

"Leave it to me. I've got fouls to burn," says Baby Bear. "I'll knock that Euro-boy's dome clean off."

Grizzly, a mountain of a senior, is one of the biggest centers in all of college basketball. And his immense size is the only reason the smaller, six-foot-nine, 260-pound DeJuan Wilkins could ever be referred to as Baby Bear. All year long, the pair had growled over Malcolm, a freshman, barking out orders. But with the Spartans' entire season now resting on Malcolm's ability to score, Grizzly and Baby Bear apparently decide to put their pride aside.

Nearing the end of regulation, a pair of pivotal Michigan State players had fouled out of the game. So Barker now points to Michael Jordan, who removes his warm-up top and gets ready to take the floor.

This isn't the Michael Jordan who won the NCAA Championship with North Carolina, six NBA Championships with the Chicago Bulls, and two Olympic gold medals. Not Air Jordan, with his "Jumpman" silhouette on his own brand of basketball shoes.

No, this is the junior benchwarmer of the same name, whose jump shot sometimes makes it look like he's applying for work as a bricklayer.

"Hey, MJ, play like the man you're named after. Not like you usually do," demands Malcolm, tugging him in close with a firm grip on the waistband of his shorts. "That means don't screw things up. Just get the rock to *me*."

"I hear you loud and clear," answers MJ, in an unsettled voice. "No heroics, just steady play. I got it."

Before he walks onto the court for overtime, Malcolm's piercing brown eyes settle on a girl in the Michigan State band. He hears the pounding rhythm of her snare and watches the drumsticks in her hands moving faster and faster, until they become a blur.

AUGUST, TWO YEARS AND SEVEN MONTHS AGO

The mercury had hit ninety-six degrees that sweltering summer day, and the sun baked the red brick of the Brewster-Douglass Houses.

It was nearly five thirty in the afternoon as Malcolm headed home from the asphalt courts, bare-chested, with a sweat-soaked T-shirt dangling from a belt loop on his cutoffs.

He pounded a basketball against the concrete, in rhythm to his steps.

Right-handed.

Left-handed.

Right-handed.

Left-handed.

The heat from the sidewalk came up through the bottoms of his kicks, until the soles of Malcolm's feet felt like they were on fire.

"Hey, Malc," called a voice from a circle of teens on the opposite corner, in the shadow of a liquor store on St. Antoine Street, one where a sheet of bulletproof glass separated the customers from the guy at the register. "It's too hot to be balling. Come chill with us."

They were dudes who Malcolm was tight with from his hood and school, mostly dressed in tank tops, shorts, and sneakers with no socks. And there were two open forty-ounce beers on the ground beside them, on either side of a metal pole from a parking meter.

They were hanging out, looking for a good time.

But there was a pair of guys with them, wearing heavy cargo pants with more pockets than you could count. Those dudes were doing business.

Malcolm threw a hand up to wave.

"My mama's birthday dinner's tonight," he hollered back, without breaking his stride. "I gotta go."

"Don't party *too* hard with the old folks!"

Malcolm wasn't an angel. He'd been involved in his share of drama during his first two years of high school. He wanted junior year to be different, though.

He'd been suspended for fighting the semester before, after a beef he had on the basketball court carried over into a classroom. And his father had to pick him up once at the station house when cops nabbed him on the street for underage drinking.

But Malcolm didn't have any real interest in watching other kids screw around, drink, or get high. He'd seen too many sweeps by the Detroit PD, who'd bust anyone within fifty feet of dudes dealing drugs. So Malcolm didn't even cross over to the other side of the street.

A half-block later, Malcolm passed another group of guys camped out around a bench. They were a little older and more serious about *business*. Malcolm recognized them, too. Only this time there weren't any greetings, just an exchange of hard looks.

At the edge of the four identical fourteen-story project buildings, younger kids were splashing in the spray from an open hydrant. Nearby, middle school girls were spinning ropes, making their own cool breeze. They were jumping double Dutch, popping out rhymes.

> Call the army, call the navy,
> Maya's gonna have a baby.
> Wrap it up in tissue paper,
> Send it down the elevator.
> Boy, girl, twins, triplets,
> Boy, girl, twins, triplets.

Without noticing, Malcolm had changed the rhythm of his dribble to match their cadence.

Over it all was the sound of rap, hip-hop, and R & B mixed together, filtering through the air. Smokey Robinson and Diana Ross, two of his mama's favorite singers, grew up in these projects. Malcolm knew that was the music she'd want to hear at her birthday dinner. And he was already thinking about putting on the CD of Smokey's "My Girl," just to hear his father sing to her—*Talkin 'bout my girl. My girl.*

As Malcolm started for Building 302, his sister, Trisha, came bounding through the front doors and headed down the concrete path towards him.

She was dressed in a gray T-shirt that read M.L.K. CRUSADERS MARCHING BAND, with five interlocking rings beneath.

"Think fast, sis," said Malcolm, sending her a chest-high pass.

Trisha was going to be a senior in September at Martin Luther King High School, where Malcolm was about to become a junior.

"What, you think ballers are the only ones with quick hands?" Trisha shot back, after cushioning the ball to a stop between her fingertips and palms. "Just remember who was the first McBride to play in front of a packed stadium—me."

The summer before, she'd taken her snare drum and gone with the band to perform at the Olympics in Beijing. They were one of a hundred high school bands invited from around the world. Trisha even played on the Great Wall of China and toured the Forbidden City, where Chinese emperors once lived.

The school raised three hundred thousand dollars in donations to make it happen. Plenty of people from the projects who couldn't afford it donated five or ten dollars out of pride, to see teens from their neighborhood do something like that.

When she got back home, the first question Malcolm had asked her was about how good the Chinese food was over there. He was disappointed as anything to find out that Trisha hadn't seen any fried rice, egg rolls, or spareribs on the whole two-week trip. Instead, she ate dumplings, roast duck, and baby octopus.

"Dinner is all ready. I made meatloaf. It's in the oven and just needs to be heated up," said Trisha. "Here's your job: set the table *after* you shower, and sign Mama's birthday card. And I don't mean just print your name. Write something nice in it and make sure you use the word *love*."

"Here's your job," Malcolm parroted her. "Where are *you* going?"

"I'm doing a favor for Ramona—watching little Sha-Sha in the water while she goes to the store."

Ramona had been Trisha's best friend since grade school. When Ramona got pregnant at fifteen, Malcolm's parents put Trisha under lock and key for a while. But so far, Trisha still seemed to have more interest in school and band practice than running around with boys.

"I'll be back in about a half hour. Now, take a gut check," Trisha said, shoving the ball hard into Malcolm's stomach.

A breath of air popped out of his lungs on impact. "Lucky you're a female, or I'd knock you flat with the next pass."

"You just make sure Mama keeps out of the kitchen while I'm gone," Trisha said from over her shoulder, walking away. "I don't want her waiting on you or Daddy, not on her b-day."

"Yeah, well, I'm not your slave either," said Malcolm. "I see that you doing favors for other people puts more work on me."

"Deal with it, baby bro!" she called out, without ever looking back. "It's not always about you!"

In a single leap, Malcolm took the three steps leading up to the building's entrance. Going through those double glass doors was like walking into a furnace, with the air inside almost too thick and heavy to breathe. He draped his T-shirt across the back of his neck and hit the buzzer to apartment 1204.

"Who's there?" asked his mama over the intercom.

It was the last time Malcolm would hear her voice that carefree.

"Me, Mama," he answered.

Malcolm felt the returning buzz in his hand and heard the lock click as he grabbed the burning-hot door handle.

Inside, his eyes scanned the rows of mailboxes built into the wall, and the new bulletin board postings—

EARN 50K A YEAR WORKING FROM HOME!

LOSE 40 LBS. FIRST MONTH, NO EXERCISE.

SATURDAY NIGHT HOUSE PARTY WITH DJ SCRIBE.

REDUCE HYPERTENSION NOW!

Then Malcolm rode an elevator alone to the twelfth floor. On the way up, he dribbled the ball one time, and the harsh echo off the metal walls pounded back at his eardrums.

When the elevator doors opened, Malcolm heard a growing commotion in the hall. From around the bend, there was loud banging on a door, and snippets of panicked voices.

"*Those were gunshots . . .*"

"*A drive-by, I think . . .*"

"*Hurt . . .*"

"*Shot . . .*"

"*Oh, God no! God, let me be wrong!*"

*"I have a first and a last name. I'm not just some passerby.
I know that some people don't like this, but they have to
understand, no matter how miserable it makes them.
There's room for Europeans (in U.S. basketball)."*

—Dražen Petrović, one of the first European players
to succeed in the NBA, elected to the Hall of Fame
posthumously after his death in a 1993 car accident

CHAPTER TWO
ROKO BACIC

7:20 P.M. (CT)

"**O**ne, two, three—teamwork!" echoes inside the circle of Trojans as coach Alvin Kennedy, a tall slender black man in his late thirties, breaks the huddle at their bench.

Then, junior Roko Bacic feels a hand on his shoulder.

Kennedy pulls him aside, looks him square in the eye, and says, "This is *your* time. We thrive on your energy. An extra five minutes is nothing for you. Be that Red Bull."

"If I'd stopped McBride on that shot, we'd be celebrating right now, cutting down the nets," says Roko, shaking his head in disgust. "That's on me."

"You couldn't have played any better defense. Just let it go," says Kennedy, gently shoving Roko onto the court. "You're the only one that's got an answer for Malcolm McBride so far. Don't let him think he's got something over you. And don't you believe it, either."

Walking onto the court with Roko is senior center Crispin Rice and senior forward Aaron Boyce.

"I forget under all this pressure—isn't basketball supposed to be fun?" Crispin asks in a serious tone, glimpsing his fiancée, Hope Daniels, in the middle of a dance routine. She's a Troy cheerleader, a stunning blonde with jade eyes and a sleek athletic body.

Before Roko can respond, Aaron, a native of New Orleans, who has more than thirty relatives and friends attending the game, points into the stands and says, "Nah, it's *their* job to have all the fun. We get to sweat it out under the microscope."

"I'm with Aaron. His family practically owns this Superdome tonight," Roko tells Crispin. "Just play loose. Your stroke will come back, C-Rice."

Then Roko swallows hard, before letting go of a long *belchhhh*.

The night before, Aaron's mother had the entire Troy team and coaching staff—nearly twenty people—over to her house for dinner. She served crawfish, gumbo, and red beans and rice. For some of the players, including Roko, it was their first taste of Cajun cooking.

"Son, what's your teammate writing down in that little notebook of his, my dinner menu?" Roko had heard Aaron's mother asking about him.

"He's a journalism major, Ma," answered Aaron, sitting a

few seats away from Roko at the kitchen table. "The Red Bull's always writing something in that book. He's practicing to be a reporter one day."

"So Mr. Red Bull Reporter, let me ask *you* a question," said Aaron's mother, setting down another platter of crawfish. "I know you're from Europe. How do you like that southern-style food they serve in Troy, Alabama?"

"I won't lie. It took my stomach some getting used to. But I've got a taste for grits now," answered Roko. "And I like the way they deep-fry everything, even the Snickers bars."

"Deep-fried candy? Well, N'awlins cooking is a different animal," she said. "It'll get your motor running hot for sure, so be careful. It's spicy enough to have you sweating before the big game."

"I'm feeling the heat already," said Roko, using a hand to fan his open mouth. "I didn't know there was hot pepper baked inside the biscuits, not until I ate three."

"That's jalapeño bread. We're full of warm little surprises down here," she said. "See, we don't have *guests* to our homes, just extended family. So if there's anything you need, you come straight to me—your brother's mother. You hear?"

Roko nodded his head, copying down a few of her words before he shut his notebook.

There wasn't enough space or chairs in the kitchen for everyone. So people were eating in almost every room of the small house and out on the front porch, too. But when Coach Kennedy made a speech in the living room, everyone did their best to cram inside or into the doorways at either end.

"When I banned cell phones and iPods from our trip to the Final Four, the idea was that it would bring us closer together. That we'd be talking and listening to each other a lot more, like a family," said Kennedy. "Mrs. Boyce's hospitality tonight has really reinforced that. Now we have a home and not just a hotel. I think she deserves a round of applause."

Near the end of the clapping and cheers, Aaron announced, "There's one more family thing. It was Ma's idea. Since Roko's parents couldn't make it from Croatia, my aunt and uncle agreed to take their place. Come on in!"

The pair made their way into the living room wearing curly red wigs.

"They'll be the only black people at the game with bright red hair!" Aaron told Roko, over a wave of laughter. "They're your new peeps!"

"It's like looking into a mirror," Roko said with a huge smile across his face, before he hugged them both.

And right now, as Roko gets into position on the court beside Malcolm McBride, he finds his surrogate family in the stands behind the Troy bench and gives them a big thumbs-up. But somehow, instead of making Roko feel better, it only makes him miss his real family even more.

April 18 (Grade 9)
Important note—this is a journal not a diary. A diary is for girls and their heartaches of love. I have no heart troubles yet because I do not have a girlfriend that is steady. This is my first time

writing in a journal. I am starting in high school
first year. My uncle Dražen said I have opinions
worth something now. But not cash money. This
journal is his idea.

He is a writer for his job. He is a journalist at a
newspaper here in Zagreb—capital city of Croatia.
Uncle Dražen said I should write in English. For
many more people can understand my words on
future dates. I study English since grade 4. The
vocabulary of mine is getting stronger and better
every day. I see US movies like <u>The Departed</u>,
<u>Friday Night Lights</u>, <u>Kill Bill</u>. I hear US music
also. Songs by Slim Shady and Snoop Dogg. So
I know how the English language sounds for
real—street real. Not like the fake Harry Potter
from the English of England. I call wizard Harry
Potter fake because no magic words can change
things. That is the lesson you learn in Croatia past
schooltime—wishes and words mean nothing.

How to start in my journal? Uncle Dražen said
from the beginning of my memory to now. Okay.
First thing I know from when I am very young is
war. In some days before grade one I am playing
alone outside my house. From nowhere there is
siren and whistling sounds through the clouds
and air to my ears. One shell explodes on a street
close by. After that I am upside down flying,
very scared, crying for my mother. But it is my

mother that grabbed me. She is carrying me to the basement of my neighbor for safe shelter from shells. I sleep that night on the floor in basement with no bathroom.

Now here is my good opinion worth something—yesterday, today, tomorrow is the same. It is like a quiet war. End of Croatia Independence War in 1995, my schoolbook states as fact. Big lie. Only true parts: No more warning sirens. No more shells. No more hiding in shelters in basements with neighbors. But war is still here in Croatia. Every day to night. War is left over. How? Much less tourists travel to here for vacation time to spend money. Few good jobs. Much drinking and drugs. War is poor people fighting for $$$. The factory job for my father? Open! Closed! Open! Closed! That is today.

But there is good things in my life too. Uncle Dražen lives in our house now with me, my mother, my father. My uncle has no spouse or child yet so I am like his son. He teaches me to play basketball—shoot, dribble, pass, defense. Always more defense. Uncle Dražen beat me last time we play 15 to 12. Future I want to play for my high school team. I practice very much with my friends after school, homework, house chores. I am almost 6 feet in height. But more inches are needed. Uncle Dražen said size of the heart is more important than

inches for basketball. Each Saturday we get up
at 4 o'clock in morning to watch Kobe, LeBron,
D-Wade play in NBA on satellite TV. But the
very best is past Michael Jordan highlight dunks
on YouTube. He is king of mad hops. I bow down
to him. Even if he is retired and old. For now I
can only touch the official 10 foot rim. My father
said basketball is for child not man. He said enjoy
while I still can, and he laugh at Uncle Dražen
for spending so much time on sport. One day I
will dunk. When I possess more inches and more
heart. I will do this before I am a grown man with
family to worry for.

September 14 (Grade 10)
My lifelong dream has become true. I made my
high school basketball team. Two days past I
went to the first tryout in our gymnasium. I was
sweating an ocean of saltwater even before the
tryout begins. There were 37 hopeful players
to fill up just 13 spots for the roster. But 10 of
those spots were taken up automatic by returning
players from last year. That meant my chances
were very poor. I missed the only two shots I took.
Clank! Clank! All nerves and no shooting touch.
But on defense I played against the senior all-star
guard with more inches and muscles than me. I

was not embarrassed by him and was able to keep him always within my arms reach.

I did not sleep a wink later that night. Like I only knew an alphabet without the ZZZZZs. I made no journal entry so I would not have to read it forever if I got cut. Uncle Dražen could see I was uptight and did not push me for details. The next day at school I am on the list of players making the first cut—from 37 down to 20. At the second tryout my defense is even better. I also made three of three shots and know that God heard my praying and guided the most difficult one into the basket. Again I had little sleep. Only this time for excitement because I know I played well. Uncle Dražen could see it in my eyes. He patted me on the back and said, "It is beautiful to feel so alive for something."

This morning I walked up to the list with my eyes closed. Then I opened them with two sets of fingers crossed. Hooray! Props to me! My name is printed number 12 of 13 in the coach's own writing. All day long school is a joy. Nothing can bring me down. At home my father shakes my hand warning that studying and chores must always come first. Uncle Dražen kisses my cheek saying he will sweep the yard every day in my place in exchange for tickets to my first professional game. When my uniform comes I will sleep in it. I will wear it under my street clothes. I have already told my mother that I will wash it myself by hand—never to let it out of my sight.

November 15 (Grade 10)

Today I made my first dunk on the official height rim during basketball practice at school. It was 10 feet of rim vs. 6 foot 2 inches of me. No problem! The sound of the basket shaking was like beautiful music to my ears. It pumped me up more than any Jay-Z beat. And I smiled after dunking for a long time without stopping until my cheeks felt sore.

When I returned home my father shook my hand and told me now I can concentrate on real life. So I waited for Uncle Dražen to arrive from his job. I dragged him to the hoops at the public park in the cold to show off. He took a picture of my new dunk skills on his cell phone and saved it to his wallpaper. We celebrated with high fives and caramel custard. He has not won against me in games of one-on-one for a while now. But I do not rub it into his face.

December 1 (Grade 10)

Yes!!! Now I will have money for dates. Uncle Dražen fixed me for Saturday work at his newspaper. My job is to load the big bundles of papers into the trucks for delivering. He said to me, "It is a job that a teenage boy can handle because your mind can be on 20 different things at one time and still do it right."

I need the money because girls such as Rosa, Teresa, and even hot-legs Valeria look at me now—and not just like a skinny scarecrow. They see me wear my team jacket and sweat suit everywhere. Those clothes are babe magnets to the highest degree, even more important than a car.

January 13 (Grade 10)

There was another gang attack in my school today. It happened in a classroom with the teacher present. I was not there. But others said four thugs from our own school ran into the room and beat Baldo M. until his head began to bleed. All because he bought a long knife from one of them and didn't pay on time. Funny/sad—it is more dangerous to have a weapon than not. That is why I do not carry one.

The gangs leave me alone because I wear the same team jacket as others. Having teammates is protection. Even my father agrees this is a worthy point of playing basketball.

February 5 (Grade 10)
Today we lost the high school championship game
of Zagreb by many points. Too many points for
me to write down forever in ink. It was the big
smackdown and blowout. We were punked to the
max! There is sadness, sorrow, and shameful
heads hanging down with all of my teammates and
me. I wear #23 for Michael Jordan. But my talent
is not up to his number. My heart is not strong
enough to be a champion yet.

All basketball season my playing time grew to
more and more minutes, being on the court and
off the bench. So I am at least happy for that.
Uncle Dražen came to clap for me, and give advice
like a second coach. He is also a second father
in my life which means much more. He said there
would be a story about the game in his newspaper.
My first time in a newspaper and I will not want to
read it because we lost by so much. Tough shits
on me!!!

February 16 (Grade 10)
Uncle Dražen has two victories to celebrate today.
One of his stories about criminal organizations
in Croatia is on the front page again. He has the
heart to tell the truth and point finger to Fat Tony
Soprano mobsters and crime family of Zagreb.
They rip off hardworking people, little by little to

add up their loot. The headlines on front pages have my uncle's name. I see it thousands of times on Saturdays before the papers leave by trucks.

Uncle Dražen's new job of editor is also an official victory now. It comes with a money raise but also another price tag. Letters and phone calls come to his office with violent threats for the truth he writes about. He told me basketball and writing is not for scared little mice. That when you lose the courage to say what you are thinking you will have nothing left. Uncle Dražen has the heart I want to grow inside of me. It is the champion's heart. He is the Michael Jordan of newspaper writing.

"Mental toughness is to physical as four is to one."

—Bobby Knight, who coached the University of Indiana
to three National Championships and won more Division
I basketball games than any other coach

CHAPTER THREE
CRISPIN RICE

7:22 P.M. (CT)

His muscles aching with fatigue, Crispin bends at the waist and lets his long arms drop, touching his fingertips to the floor. Even if he'd downed a gallon of Gatorade on the sideline, the dehydration from playing nearly all forty minutes of regulation time would still have him cramping up.

But that's Crispin's role right now—to fight off the exhaustion and all of the pain, both physical and mental, that goes with it.

Crispin is the Trojans' only legitimate big man, their one answer to the Spartans' superior size and strength. And he has felt the weight of that load all night long, practically carrying Michigan State's Grizzly Bear Cousins on his back.

There are five opposing pairs of players on the floor. Four of them have taken up positions around the circumference of the circle at center court, with Crispin and Grizzly in the middle of them all, preparing for the jump ball to begin overtime. So Crispin straightens himself from his deep stretch, staring up at Grizzly, who has two inches and more than thirty pounds on him.

"Hey, don't forget how we started out this game," announces Grizzly to his teammates in green. "With a little something sweet for *our* girl."

Malcolm chimes in, "That's right. I don't care if it takes longer than we planned. We're walking away with everything these guys have got. Their game, their pride, *and* their Hope."

Then Grizzly, Malcolm, and Baby Bear each blow a kiss in the direction of Hope Daniels.

It's exactly how the trio of Spartans began the game.

That's when Crispin's blood begins to boil.

"After we win, you losers can kiss my ass," says Crispin, whose face turns as red as his jersey. "You guys don't know where the line is."

"This is war. There is no line," snaps Malcolm. "We're playing for keeps."

"There's low class and there's no class," says Roko, from his position next to Malcolm. "I haven't made up my mind which one you Spartans are."

"Definitely no class, especially Mr. One and Done over there," says Aaron Boyce, jutting his chin towards Malcolm. "I hear he can't find any *class*—on the court or in his school."

The ref blows his whistle, putting an end to all of the talk.

Then he tosses the ball up between both centers, higher than either one can reach.

Though Crispin can't out-jump Grizzly, that sudden jolt of anger has his adrenaline really pumping. He times his leap for the ball perfectly, tapping it over to Roko.

The Trojans advance the basketball from left to right.

Aaron gets open along the baseline for a jumper, and Roko instantly zips him a pass. Crispin is battling hard for position beneath the basket. Arms are flailing all around him, and the back of his hand scrapes across Grizzly's sharp stubble.

Both teams are determined to score the first basket of over-time. It shows the will to win, putting the other squad in an immediate hole.

Aaron's release is smooth as silk.

Crispin somehow wedges his body past Grizzly's as his eyes follow the shot out of Aaron's hand. The ball goes halfway down into the basket before it rattles back out, with Crispin reeling in the rebound at the front of the rim.

And he suddenly feels the confidence of a shot that he can't miss.

Stuffing the ball home with a resounding "Umph," Crispin gives the Trojans a 66–64 lead. Then he glares back at Grizzly, pushing his lips together.

On the way down court, Crispin slaps hands with his team-mates, making eye contact with Hope for the first time since the game began more than two hours ago. It is a passing glance with which neither seems comfortable.

From that morning's national newspaper:

HOPE OF TROY HAS TROJANS STREAKING

NEW ORLEANS, La. — Move over, Helen of Troy. The face that supposedly launched a thousand ships during the Trojan War has some spirited modern-day competition in Troy University cheerleader Hope Daniels, aka "Hope of Troy."

Back in early February, Hope was busy cheering her heart out for the home team, the Troy University Trojans, who trailed by 2 points in the final few seconds. Hope's beau, senior center Crispin Rice, blew her a kiss as he stepped onto the court. An instant later, Rice hit a 40-foot desperation 3-point basket at the buzzer to give Troy a dramatic victory. Instead of celebrating with his teammates, Rice raced towards the sidelines. He got down on one knee and proposed to Hope. She accepted. The replay of the game-winning basket/marriage proposal was seen on practically every sports highlight show in the country and has so far recorded more than one million hits on YouTube.

"It was a magical moment for me and Crispin," said Hope, a senior majoring in business management. "This irresistible force just swept us up. It's been an incredible ride, and we've gotten to share it with so many people."

Since Hope accepted Crispin's proposal, Troy hasn't lost a single basketball game. Heading into tonight's semifinal matchup at the Final Four with Michigan State, it has been nine consecutive wins and counting. Two more victories and the Trojans will claim an improbable National Championship.

After Troy's first-round upset over Wisconsin, their first NCAA Tournament win ever, the national media began calling Daniels "Hope of Troy."

Helen of Troy, a daughter of Zeus and the most beautiful woman in the world, was a Spartan queen stolen away by Paris, a Trojan prince. The Spartans went to battle for her return, beginning the Trojan War detailed in Homer's epic poems, the *Iliad* and the *Odyssey*. Now that the Michigan State Spartans are playing the Trojans of Troy, the comparison of Hope to Helen has garnered even more attention.

"She certainly inspires me," said Crispin Rice, a health and human services major, who at 6 feet 10 inches tall towers over his 5-foot-7-inch fiancée. "I want to play my best for her, every time."

Despite the string of Trojan victories, Crispin

Rice, whose teammates nicknamed him "Snap-Crackle-Pop" for his ability to shoot a basketball, has been in a scoring slump lately.

"I guess there's been a little bit of pressure on me, thinking about the engagement and all," said Rice. "But I'm confident I'll get my touch back."

Of course, Crispin Rice is optimistic. He has Hope on his side.

The pair will set a wedding date sometime after the NCAA Tournament.

"I've failed over and over and over again in my life, and that is why I succeed."

—Michael Jordan, considered by many to be the greatest basketball player of all time, despite being cut from his high school varsity team as a sophomore

CHAPTER FOUR
MICHAEL JORDAN

7:24 P.M. (CT)

MJ knows he's not the focus on offense for the Spartans, and maybe not even a second or third option in the minds of his teammates. But that doesn't matter to him. He still holds on to a scorer's mentality—that he can drain any open shot if he puts himself in the right spot or the ball bounces his way.

On Michigan State's first possession of overtime, Malcolm jukes left with his dribble. When Roko commits in that direction on defense, Malcolm jets back to his right, where MJ mans the corner.

MJ steps back, giving Malcolm plenty of room to operate.

Roko throws his legs into high gear to catch up.

MJ sees Baby Bear step squarely in front of Roko to set a screen. As the Croatian runs into that brick wall of flesh, the

Trojan guarding MJ darts after Malcolm, leaving MJ wide open for a mid-range jumper.

Instantaneously, MJ feels his mouth go dry and the sweat starting on his palms.

Planting his feet firmly on the floor, MJ extends his hands forward, waiting for the ball. Malcolm sees him. His eyes look right into MJ's.

But the pass never comes.

Instead, Malcolm forces up a shot with two defenders closing in on him.

In a heartbeat, MJ pushes through the curtain of curse words in his mind, and he rushes towards the rim to rebound Malcolm's miss.

The ball hangs in the air, right in front of MJ.

But just as he reaches for it, Baby Bear comes barreling to the rim from behind.

The pair battle for the same rebound, with the ball going off MJ's leg and out of bounds.

The ref points directly at MJ, slapping at his pant leg. Then he thrusts an arm towards the opposite basket, like a sucker punch to MJ's midsection, awarding Troy possession.

"Don't dog your own teammate for the rock!" Malcolm explodes at MJ. "You're balling for our team, not theirs! Get your head out of your ass!"

Baby Bear has the same snarling look for MJ, minus the sharp words.

MJ sucks it all up and swallows that tongue-lashing. He's not about to fight with his teammates. Not while he's still trying to find his place on the court.

Then MJ heads back on defense, muttering, "It's all about trust, Malc. Just pass me the ball when I'm open. That's all."

ON A CABLE SPORTS NETWORK PROVIDING LIVE UPDATES FROM THE FINAL FOUR

Announcer: There's no doubt that most of you are familiar with this iconic name. Maybe you're not so familiar with the Michigan State player who currently bears it in college basketball. He's normally a reserve, spending most of his time on the bench. But due to a pair of Spartans fouling out earlier tonight, junior Michael Jordan is seeing important minutes on the court as I speak. Let's get to know him better through an encore presentation of Rachel Adams's award-winning interview series, *One-on-One*.

On screen, Rachel Adams (screen left), holding a small pile of index cards, and Michael Jordan (screen right) are sitting on stools, facing each other. Erected between them is a life-size cardboard cutout of the famed Michael Jordan, with one hand on his hip in a Superman pose and a basketball tucked beneath the other arm. In the background is a darkened gymnasium basketball court.

Rachel Adams: Tell me, honestly, what's it like for a basketball player to grow up with the name Michael Jordan?

Michael: It can be hard, real hard. How can I explain it? I guess it would be like if your name was Oprah and you had one of those TV talk shows. How could you ever measure up? *(Adams laughs)* It's probably harder on me having the name Michael Jordan *(glancing over at the cardboard cutout)*, because I love the game of basketball so much, since I was a little kid.

Adams: So it's safe to say that there was a lot of pressure involved, a lot of unrealistic expectations?

Michael: Think about it—I had this name to deal with even before I really learned how to play basketball. When I was, like, seven years old and couldn't reach the rim yet with a shot, people were saying, "Hey, your name's Michael Jordan; you're not supposed to miss." That's pressure. I'd eat breakfast every morning and a guy with my name was on the Wheaties box. If I grew up playing chess or piano, it probably wouldn't matter. People wouldn't make such a big deal out of it. They'd never say, "There goes Michael Jordan to his piano lesson. He must play piano as great as the real Michael Jordan plays basketball." It probably wouldn't come into their minds.

Adams: But Michael *(pointing a finger at him)*, you *are* the real Michael Jordan, right? There's nothing fake about you. I mean, it is your name.

Michael: That's true. I have to remember that. Thanks for reminding me. I am the real MJ *(pinching himself on the arm)*. Yeah, that's me. The only Michael Jordan I know. And a least I've still got my hair *(looking at the bald image of Jordan)*. It's one thing I do have over *him.*

Adams: What do you think people expect from you because of that name?

Michael: I think they expect me to dominate every basketball game I play in. That I'm going to score a lot of points and win championships. Oh yeah, and that I'm going to dunk on everybody all the time. *(Screen cuts to a famous video clip of Michael Jordan dunking from the free-throw line during an NBA All-Star Game dunk contest)* Or people come up to me and ask, "Is Michael Jordan your father? Are you his son?" That's always a good one.

Adams: What do you tell them when they ask that—"Is Michael Jordan your father?"

Michael: I mostly say, "I wish Michael Jordan was my father, because that means my father would still be alive." Don't get me wrong—I love my mom. But she got remarried a few years back to a guy with three kids of his own, all younger than me. So she's been busy helping to raise them. It got a little lonely sometimes, like I'd been forgotten. So I'd sit and wonder what it would be like if my dad was still here.

As heartfelt music begins to play, on screen appears this Michael Jordan shooting alone in a gymnasium, wearing a green Michigan State

Spartans warm-up jersey. Rachel Adams's voice is heard over the video.

Adams: In truth, this Michael Jordan never really knew his father. Anthony Jordan split up with Michael's mother, Justine, several months after Michael was born. A few months later, Anthony Jordan was killed in a car accident. But before he left Michael's life, he gave his son the name of his athletic hero. He also left behind a box with some possessions—among them an old basketball. That ball became one of young Michael's favorite things to play with.

The broadcast cuts back to the interview.

Michael: I dribbled that ball around everywhere growing up. I played with it so much the grips wore off and it became all smooth. I still have the ball at home. I let my stepsiblings touch it, but they're not allowed to take it out of the house. I'll probably keep it forever.

Adams: Interestingly enough, I understand Michael Jordan isn't your hero.

Michael: No, President Barack Obama is. He's my hero.

Adams: Tell me why, Michael.

Michael: Well, besides being the first black president, I read that Barack Obama only met his father a few times, because his dad was working as a diplomat in another country. Obama met him one Christmas when his father was visiting the U.S. I know that he got a basketball as a present. So President Obama is sort of like me: we both got basketballs to remember our fathers by. Anyway, we're both left-handed. And I've seen some of the president's game on the news clips. It's kind of like mine—scrappy with a little bit of a jump shot.

Adams: And do you realize what happens, Michael, if your Michigan State Spartans win the National Championship?

Michael: Yeah, the team will get invited to the White House to meet President Obama *(a smile appearing on his face)*.

Adams: What would you say to President Obama? Would you tell him about the similarities in your lives?

Michael: Nah, he wouldn't want to hear all of that. I'd probably just want to shake his hand and maybe take a picture with him.

Adams: If this Michael Jordan magically came to life *(glancing at the cutout)*, what would you say to him?

Michael: I'd say how all of his success has made it rough for me. I don't think he'd have much sympathy, though. He's a super-tough competitor. He'd probably tell me to just work harder at everything.

Adams: Michael, you're not a starter on the Michigan State team, and you more than likely won't be turning pro. What do you want to do after graduation?

Michael: I'm majoring in media and communications. Maybe one day I'll have a job like yours. So this interview could be good practice for me, on-the-job training.

Adams: Now, Michael, I have to ask you this last question. If you ever had a son, would you name him Michael Jordan?

Michael: I don't know *(resting his cleft chin in the palm of his right hand)*. I can't really call it. Not if he ever wanted to be a basketball player, I wouldn't.

The broadcast cuts back to the studio announcer.

Announcer: It is reported that Hall of Famer Michael Jordan is at the Final Four in New Orleans this weekend to see his alma mater, North Carolina, play in the second semifinal game tonight against Duke. So far, there's no word on whether the two Michael Jordans have gotten the opportunity to meet each other.

"I was brought up in this part of Detroit that they used to call the ghetto. . . . My father worked hard, but we were still very poor; and I didn't want anybody arguing about money, so I became the entertainer—the one who wanted everyone to be happy. I didn't want there to be any problems."

—Diana Ross, famed Motown recording artist whose family moved into the Brewster-Douglass Housing Projects in her early teens

CHAPTER FIVE
MALCOLM McBRIDE

7:25 P.M. (CT)

Trailing by a bucket, even the offensive-minded Malcolm is determined to clamp down on defense, denying his man the ball.

"Nothing for you," Malcolm tells Roko, as he cuts him off from receiving a pass. "If I wanted to make it happen, you'd never touch the rock. You're lucky my game's about putting points on the board or I'd be living inside your jersey."

The Spartans' defense smothers the Trojans' attack. With the thirty-five-second shot clock about to expire, Troy is forced to heave up a bad, off-balance shot.

Grizzly snatches the rebound, clearing out space with a vicious swinging elbow.

Then Malcolm rushes over to him to claim the ball.

Stalking the sidelines, Coach Barker signals a play by raising a fist into the air.

Malcolm grimaces at the sight of it, grinding his teeth in disgust.

He can't believe the play isn't for him.

"I wouldn't call your number, either," mocks Roko, as Malcolm brings the ball up court. "It's already too much about you. You don't have teammates. You have babysitters."

Malcolm glares at Roko's red hair and uniform, and then drops his shoulder like a bull about to charge.

The rest of the Spartans are following Barker's call.

But halfway through the arranged set, Malcolm blows off the play, attacking Roko one-on-one instead.

Barker throws his arms up in frustration, turning his back to the court. Even if Malcolm could see him, it wouldn't have any effect.

Malcolm's only focus is on finding a clear path to the basket or creating one for himself. Besides, Malcolm knows that Barker won't bench him. This is *his* overtime. *He's* the one who has carried the Spartans this far.

Bursting past Roko, Malcolm doesn't have a planned move. He's playing by touch and feel. And what comes out of him is a high, arching shot—a running teardrop floater in the lane.

Crispin leaps to block it, but the ball just clears his fingertips before nestling into the net.

The score is knotted 66–66, with 2:40 left in overtime.

But Malcolm isn't done. He reads Crispin's disappointment at narrowly missing the block. He sees him lose concentration and get careless with the inbound pass to Roko. That's when Malcolm darts in front, stealing the ball.

Backing off with his prize, Malcolm hesitates for a second, selling the idea to Roko and Crispin that he'll wait for his teammates to regroup on offense.

Then Malcolm heads for the hoop at full throttle, past the suckered pair.

Roko can only rake him across the arm, trying to stop an easy score. But Malcolm's momentum and strength are too much. He drags Roko with him to the basket and scores anyway.

The ref raises his arm for a foul on Roko.

Then he lashes his wrist straight down to signal the basket counts, too.

A wave of green rocks the Superdome, starting at the Spartans' bench.

Even Coach Barker is now clapping for Malcolm, straining what's left of his voice with approval. "Big-time play! Big-time!"

Before Malcolm heads to the foul line for a free throw, he stops in front of a TV camera beneath the basket. He stares into the lens, beating at his chest with a clenched fist. Malcolm hits himself harder and harder, until he feels the sting of those blows deep inside.

AUGUST, TWO YEARS AND SEVEN MONTHS AGO

The elevator doors sprang shut behind him as Malcolm turned the corner and saw it was his apartment door that the neighbors were pounding on.

Soon his parents were out in the hall, too.

"Malcolm, come here, baby!" shrieked his mama, shaking out both of her hands at the wrists, like that motion was the only thing keeping the rest of her body and mind together. "Stand by me. I don't want to lose sight of you, too. Not right now."

And that wait for the elevator to come back again was pure torture.

"Damn it, this elevator is slow as shit!" raged Malcolm's father, slamming the button with his fist. "Come on! Where is it?"

"Stop, please! You'll break it!" hollered Malcolm's mama. "I need to see if my daughter is all right!"

Malcolm thought about jetting down the twelve flights of stairs. But deep inside, he didn't know if he could face whatever had happened out there alone.

When the elevator finally arrived, Malcolm, his parents, Ramona's grandparents, and some other neighbors all piled into it, almost on top of one another.

"This can't be happening," said Malcolm's mama, hysterical. "She was just here, safe in the house. Lord, please let it be someone else, some criminal who deserves it."

With every floor that passed, Malcolm felt his heart sinking further down into his shoes.

Once they hit the lobby, Malcolm could hear the sickening

sound of sirens twisting through the streets, getting closer.

Outside, through a crowd of people, Malcolm saw EMTs kneeling beside a girl wearing a gray T-shirt.

It was Trisha.

The EMTs were working feverishly, pumping at her chest and giving her oxygen.

Malcolm had never felt smaller or more helpless in his entire life.

His father was on his knees, praying in the street.

"Help her, Lord. Please, I'm begging—" was all his father got out before he broke down sobbing.

It was the first time Malcolm had ever seen his father cry.

Then, after a few minutes, the EMTs suddenly stopped. They pulled a white sheet over Trisha's bloodstained face and lifted her lifeless body into the ambulance.

That gut check Trisha had given Malcolm maybe ten minutes ago, shoving the basketball hard into his stomach, turned into a huge empty hole that passed right through him.

"Why aren't they helping my baby anymore? Why?" screamed Malcolm's mama, as neighbors rushed to hold her up.

Malcolm's legs became like rubber, as he wavered back and forth between tears and searing anger.

Without a basketball to cling to, Malcolm threw his arms around his mama.

He felt an earthquake of emotions building inside her—the kind of rumbling that could have brought the Brewster-Douglass Houses crashing down to the ground.

It was all Malcolm could do to hold on.

•　•　•

Later on, at the hospital, Malcolm and his parents were told by doctors that Trisha had been struck in the right temple by a bullet. And that it had probably killed her instantly.

It was the hardest thing Malcolm ever had to hear.

The cops called it a "stray" bullet, one from a battle over which crew would run the projects' most profitable drug spots. But Malcolm didn't need the police to explain anything. He walked those streets every day.

In all, the cops counted the casings of seven shots fired from a moving car. Two of them ended up in the body of a teenage dealer on a bench twenty yards from the hydrant where all of those kids were splashing, where Trisha was minding little Sha-Sha. Only those bullets didn't touch the lives of Malcolm and his family.

The few witnesses who weren't afraid to talk told the police that the shots came from a black Acura with tinted windows. But nobody got a good look at the shooter's face, or the car's license plate number.

There was no birthday dinner that night or talk of food in Malcolm's house for days. And Malcolm couldn't remember hearing any music again until the Martin Luther King High School Crusaders Marching Band played "Wind Beneath My Wings" at Trisha's funeral.

At the cemetery, Ramona came up from behind Malcolm and threw her arms around him. "I feel like this is all my fault," sobbed Ramona. "If I didn't ask her to mind my daughter, she'd still be here."

Malcolm wanted to scream at her, *That's right! This is all on you!* But he didn't. Instead, he broke free from Ramona's grasp and tossed a handful of dirt into Trisha's grave, on top of her coffin.

That night in her bedroom, Malcolm heard the same *tutt* sound the dirt had made every time he dropped a finger onto the skin of his sister's snare drum. He listened to it, still angry as hell at Ramona, and hating every bit of the world he could see from the window.

No one was ever arrested over Trisha's death.

Inside of a week, drugs were being dealt again from that same bench.

Malcolm couldn't walk past without losing his temper, wanting to throw down with anyone who was doing business there. Ten days after Trisha's funeral, one of those dealers shot him a challenging look, and Malcolm couldn't hold back anymore.

"Think I'm scared of that weak-ass ice grill? Maybe things are going to get evened up, big-time!" Malcolm hollered, nearly squeezing the air out of the orange basketball between his palms. "It doesn't matter if dudes are responsible for my sister or not! Sometimes being in the wrong place is good enough!"

"Better stick to b-ball," the guy said in a cold voice, before taking a long drag on a cigarette and blowing smoke from his nostrils. "This is no game. Shit's for real out here. Lots of families lose more than one kid to these streets."

"Yeah, maybe *your* mama's going to be the one crying tonight," said Malcolm, stepping forward. "'Cause mine's cried enough."

That's when another one of that crew put an arm around the guy, pulling him away.

"Forget about it, man. Let's walk for a few," he said to his partner. "There's already too much heat. Last thing we need is another chalk outline. It's bad for our pockets."

As they left, Malcolm hocked up a wad of phlegm and spit it on the ground where they'd been standing.

"Five guys on the court working together can achieve more than five talented individuals who come and go as individuals."

—Kareem Abdul-Jabbar, who played on three National Collegiate Championship teams at UCLA, won six NBA Championships and MVPs, and scored the most career points in NBA history

CHAPTER SIX
ROKO BACIC

7:26 P.M. (CT)

Roko is kicking himself as Malcolm sets his feet at the foul line.

He's pissed because he should have known better—that Malcolm wasn't about to wait for anyone, or pass the ball off, after making that steal.

"My bad," Roko calls out to his teammates. "If I was going to foul, I should have knocked his ass down so he couldn't score."

"Yeah, you keep on believing that's possible, because I sure as hell don't," says Malcolm, before the ref sends him the ball.

That's when Roko realizes he needs to change his thinking. That he needs to fight off every instinct to see the game the way he was taught to play it.

If he's going to stop Malcolm, Roko needs to see the game through Malcolm's eyes. And maybe the rest of the Spartans' eyes, too. Because they've probably learned to see things the same selfish way after playing an entire season with Malcolm.

"Thirty-two, Red Bull! Thirty-two, Red Bull! That's what we run next!" screams the willowy Kennedy, catching Roko's eye with a subtle wink.

Now Roko understands that Kennedy's thinking is the same as his.

After Malcolm's made free throw, the Spartans lead 69–66.

Roko brings the ball up court.

Malcolm gets into a defensive stance, bending low at the knees and slapping both of his palms against the floor, challenging Roko to dribble past.

Roko purposefully eyes Malcolm, and no one else.

Every Michigan State defender has heard Kennedy's play call with Roko's name and number attached. They're all waiting for Roko to take the ball to the basket, ready to tattoo the rock's WILSON logo onto his forehead.

Roko puts his head down. With a burst of speed, he drives towards the hoop.

Both Grizzly and Baby Bear come flying off their men.

Roko can hear their footsteps rushing towards him. Suddenly, he pulls up, spotting Aaron Boyce alone behind the three-point line. He feeds him the ball and Aaron buries the shot.

The game is tied 69–69, with just a little more than two minutes remaining in overtime.

Then Roko punches the air around him with a clenched fist

as the big base drum in the Trojan band punctuates that three-pointer—*Boom! Boom! Boom!*

May 23 (Grade 11)

There is no more sun. The sky over Zagreb is black. Uncle Dražen was murdered. He was killed by a car bomb. Everyone knows it was done by organized crime, by miserable mafia type people that don't deserve to live. He was blown up outside of the newspaper office at 6 o'clock tonight. My tears like a storm have not stopped since I learned the news from my father. Sadness is not close to the description of how I feel. I am totally empty inside. The biggest hole in the world is in my heart.

My mother did not want me to go down there. But I had to see it with my own two eyes. I saw Uncle Dražen's blue car turned charcoal black. It was melted down to metal bones like a burned out skeleton on the street. The smell of fire was heavy in the air. It is in my nose even now and will not leave. That same fire is burning in my blood to get revenge. A lifetime in prison is not enough for those bastard criminals. My father said there is no body of his brother left to bury. No body of his left to pray over. I know Uncle Dražen's spirit can not burn. His soul can not burn.

I hope the criminals that did this evil murder

burn in hell for eternal days and nights. How do
we know it was these criminals? A week ago they
shoved a gun in my uncle's face and told him to
write no more about them. He refused because
he is a champion. Another reporter was beat with
a baseball bat by the same types. There was no
work for me last Saturday at the newspaper. Now
I understand why. Uncle Dražen wanted to protect
me from possible harm, from violence of thugs.
My father said we can not trust the police because
some of them are owned by Croatian mafia. They
are on the criminals' payroll for a second job.
He said that maybe we are not safe in this house.
My father now has his gun by his side for the
protection of us. Like my uncle Dražen, I will not
be scared of mafia terrorists. Not today. Not
tomorrow. I will always speak my mind and have
respect for the opinions of others. When I hold my
basketball I feel Uncle Dražen close by. Now he
will always be part of my game. He will be part of
my strength and part of my heart.

My mother wants me to leave Croatia. She
wants me to finish high school in the US with my
cousins living there. I am not sure. My father says
I am old enough to decide my own life. I don't want
to run away from what Uncle Dražen started. But
the future here in Zagreb is dark. It is filled with
as much smoke and fire as outside the newspaper

office tonight. I will always keep this journal for myself and for my memory of beloved Uncle Dražen. I will miss him forever with my tears, my heart, and my soul.

August 12 (Entering Grade 12)
Today ends my first week living in the US. Big news flash—the city of Montgomery, Alabama, is not Zagreb. It is total culture shock. Even the US movies and music I know do not give me the answers to everything. There are other Croatians here besides my cousins, aunts, and uncles. But it is still a new world to me—one without my parents who stayed in Zagreb to watch over the house my great-grandfather built with his own two hands. I pray they are safe. My father says the move will force me to grow up faster. I say nothing will ever do that more than the murder of Uncle Dražen.

I am living with the sister of my mother and her husband. Their four children are all younger than me. The three girls are ages 6, 9, and 11. They are almost babies compared to me and still play with dolls. My boy cousin is 12. He has no interest in basketball or any other sports. Instead he plays the violin. I share a bedroom with him, except for when he practices his music lessons. Then the bedroom belongs 100% to him and I would rather sleep in the doghouse outside. It has been 95 degrees or more here every day so far. And I am melting in the heat and humidity like a redheaded Popsicle.

There are public basketball courts just five blocks from my new house. On the good side, the courts are close enough to walk to. On the bad side, I have already learned that five blocks is a long way to run from angry players. *Note to myself—when returning trash talk do not use the words "make you my little bitch." **I am no Slim Shady here. I have no real friends yet, just some enemies on the basketball court. **

"What happens is, when you're good at something, you spend a lot of time with it. People identify you with that sport, so it becomes part of your identity."

—Mike Krzyzewski, who coached Duke to four NCAA Championships

CHAPTER SEVEN
CRISPIN RICE

7:27 P.M. (CT)

Crispin can hear the *thud* of Grizzly's backside and shoulders slamming into him, carving out space beneath the basket. This deep into the game, there's hardly any pain attached to it anymore. Crispin's body is nearly numb from the abuse.

That just makes him even braver.

It's like staring down a dentist's drill with your mouth full of Novocain.

Those extra thirty pounds of muscle on Grizzly are still doing the job, but they've lost most of their biting sting.

Then, bracing for another collision, Crispin feels his left sneaker slide out from underneath him. A slick sweat spot on the floor gives Grizzly all the advantage he needs. Crispin goes even more off balance with a subtle hip from Grizzly, and the Spartans get the ball into their center's huge paws.

Crispin hustles back into position, putting his arms straight up in the air to defend against Grizzly's short jumper.

Their chests barely bump together as the ball caroms off the rim.

The ref whistles Crispin for a foul, his fourth of the game. One more and he's gone, with no one else near his size on the Trojans' bench for a replacement.

On the sideline, Coach Kennedy goes ballistic at the ref, screaming, "He's standing straight up! He's entitled to that space! Look at him!"

Crispin freezes in place, arms over his head, pleading his case. "How is *this* a foul? Tell me. How?"

But the ref walks away, ignoring them both.

Grizzly sinks the first of two free throws, giving the Spartans a 70–69 lead. Then Kennedy calls time-out, pounding his right palm on top of the extended fingers of his left hand to make a T, as if the ref's head was on a chopping block between them.

Inside the Trojans' huddle, Kennedy calms himself enough to call the next offensive play. Then he turns to Crispin and says, "Don't worry about fouling out. I don't care if I have to send a midget out there to take your place. Step up to every challenge. You don't ever want to lose backing down and have to carry that around with you. There's a minute thirty-two on the clock. But I promise you, life is a hell of a lot longer than that. So stand tall."

"I won't sidestep a thing, Coach," says Crispin. "I'll take it all head-on."

As the Trojans walk back onto the court, their cheerleaders are performing acrobatics.

Crispin sees Hope smiling for the crowd, standing on the shoulders of a pair of muscular guys from the pep squad. Then they toss her high into the air with her pom-poms waving, before she lands softly in their arms.

MARCH, THREE WEEKS AGO

FLYING SUSHI—that was the name across the front of Crispin's helmet as he fastened his chin strap and then revved the throttle high.

He could feel the vibrations running up his spine and the horsepower surging through his body. Then his heel hit the kickstand. He pulled away from the restaurant with two full orders bungeed in behind him. As he took off through the streets of Troy, balancing his six-foot-ten-inch frame on that red moped scooter, he never felt more like a giant sitting on top of the world.

The Trojans had just won their first two NCAA Tournament games, just four shy of a National Championship.

They'd arrived back on campus the night before with nearly the entire student body cheering for them. There was a wild celebration at the fountain with the Trojan statue on the quad. Everyone was dressed in red. There were banners, and bottles of beer right out in the open, and the Trojan band played the school's fight song over and over. And when Crispin locked lips with Hope, people started chanting, *"Hope of Troy! Hope of Troy!"*

Crispin was beat tired now. He'd gotten up early for classes and spent half the day catching up on missed assignments. But working the four to eight o'clock dinner shift meant good tip money. He could pocket maybe sixty dollars delivering for the only Chinese/Japanese takeout place in the city.

Crispin couldn't afford to pass up on that kind of cash.

He was hell-bent on saving enough money for Hope's engagement ring. He'd proposed without one, on the spur of the moment, after making that game-winning basket a month back.

In the five months they'd been dating, Crispin and Hope hadn't talked about getting married. But the idea crept into Crispin's mind a few days before he popped the question, after they'd seen a movie together where the characters got married on a whim in Las Vegas.

"Could you ever see us doing something crazy like that, running off to Vegas?" Crispin asked her on the walk back to the campus from the theater, with his arm around Hope's shoulder to protect her from a chill in the night air.

"You mean, to elope?" she answered, snuggling closer to him. "My parents would kill me. I think my mom's been planning my wedding since the day I was born. But I've got to admit, it was spontaneous. That's a big part of being romantic—keeping things fresh."

When they'd started dating, Hope made a point about wanting things to remain casual.

"My last boyfriend was really possessive and controlling," she'd told Crispin the second or third time they'd hung out together. "He'd even sneak my cell out of my purse to see who'd been calling me. I just like my freedom now, knowing I'm not boxed into anything."

But from the very beginning of their relationship, Crispin felt like they were meant for each other. He loved Hope's smile and sense of humor. She was the only girl he knew who liked belches and eating beef jerky. And Crispin loved her high-pitched laugh, which made her sound like a little kid. And whenever he heard it, it made him laugh, too.

Hope didn't seem to care about getting expensive gifts, though her parents were loaded and she used a weekly allowance to treat herself to lots of designer clothes. Crispin never spent a lot of money on Hope, because he didn't have much—his working-class parents couldn't afford to give him a fat allowance. Their dates were mostly to the movies or eating burgers at cheap diners, like Mel's with the old-fashioned soda fountain at the counter. Even when Crispin brought her flowers, he'd usually picked them from some garden himself.

So Crispin was shocked when Hope pitched a fit over not getting a diamond engagement ring.

He'd seen her have blowups before—usually screaming about a professor over a low grade, or the cheerleading coach for not featuring her in a particular dance routine. But this was the first one aimed at him.

It was on the day after Crispin proposed at the game, once all of the reporters and TV cameras had gotten their feel-good story and disappeared.

"I talked to my mother this morning, and she's absolutely right—how can I take this marriage proposal seriously without a ring?" said Hope, as they waited to share a chef's salad at Mel's. "How do I know you're really committed to me? That you won't change your mind in a week and leave me looking like a fool in front of half the country, on *TMZ* and *Extra*?"

Hearing that was like a sharp elbow to Crispin's ribs. Only this wasn't a basketball game, and he hadn't thought of Hope as the opposition before.

Crispin never winced or wiped the sympathetic look off his face.

"When I asked you to marry me, that was from the heart, not a store," Crispin said calmly, trying to hide his annoyance.

He could see that Hope was getting even more upset, shifting around in her chair like she might get up any second and walk out. That scared Crispin. He reached across the table and took her hand, trying to get her to relax. Nearly everyone knew they were engaged. He didn't want to screw it up in less than a day.

"If that's what you want, I'll get you a ring you can be proud of," he conceded. "I'll buy you one with the biggest diamond you ever saw."

"That's not the point. It doesn't have to be huge," Hope said with an attitude, as if she was looking to pick a fight with Crispin. "It just has to show people that we're committed to each other."

Crispin was completely thrown.

What's up with her? he wondered.

He was giving Hope what she wanted, but she still wasn't happy.

Later that day, they checked out a downtown jewelry store together.

Hope didn't see a ring she liked that cost less than five thousand dollars. And Crispin got pissed off at the salesman, who kept trying to steer Hope towards even more expensive rings.

"It's going to take me at least five or six months to save up that kind of money," Crispin told her when the salesman moved away to help another customer. "You really want to wait that long?"

"If I'm going to wear a ring for the rest of my life, I want it to be the right one," said Hope. "I don't want to look at it every day wishing it was something else."

Crispin had already been delivering Flying Sushi for a few months. At the end of every shift, he'd bring Hope her favorite— an order of eel rolls with seaweed and wasabi on the side. But tonight, Hope told him not to bother—that she'd be grabbing a quick dinner with friends.

And as tired as Crispin was from the basketball, celebrating, and schoolwork, he was out making deliveries to buy Hope that ring.

"Hey, Flying Sushi! Win the tournament!" somebody screamed at him from a passing car. "Go Troy! Woo-hoo!"

Crispin hit his horn in response—*beep, beep, beep*.

He usually had to explain to customers why a nearly seven-foot-tall white kid was delivering Chinese and Japanese food, instead of an Asian.

"Why the hell not?" was his standard answer. "One of the chefs in our kitchen is short and Mexican."

Most people would howl at that response, thinking it was a joke.

Only Crispin knew it was absolutely true.

But at his first stop, the talk wasn't about any of that.

It was all about the NCAA Tournament and the Trojans' winning streak.

"Think we can keep winning, C-Rice?" asked the man who answered the door. "It's like a dream come true for this city. My wife and I graduated from Troy almost ten years ago. But the team was never this good. That fiancée of yours, Hope of Troy, is our good luck charm. Give her a big kiss for me, will you?"

Before Crispin left, he posed for a photo with the man's wife and three kids, all holding up their fingers in the V sign for victory.

Crispin loved every second of it, and his tip was twice what he'd expected.

His second stop that afternoon was at a downtown apartment building, next to a leather boutique where Hope had once dragged him so she could shop for Italian boots.

He chained his moped to a parking meter and climbed the stoop.

"Flying Sushi," Crispin said into the intercom, before the customer buzzed him inside.

By the time he reached the third floor, the tiny elevator that took him upstairs smelled like a combination platter of beef and broccoli and spicy string beans in garlic sauce.

The older woman who answered the door looked up at him with her eyes rolling higher and higher. But she didn't seem to know anything about Troy basketball, so there wasn't much conversation.

As Crispin waited for the elevator back down, counting his tip, he heard a guy and girl laughing from inside another apartment.

He stood there frozen for an instant, confused, like his body and mind were suddenly in two different places. Then he moved closer to that apartment door.

The next time Crispin heard them—*hee, hee, hee, hee*—he was positive the girl's high-pitched laugh belonged to Hope.

CHAPTER EIGHT
MICHAEL JORDAN

7:30 P.M. (CT)

MJ fights for the rebound as Grizzly's second free throw glances off the rim.

The ball is rolling loose on the floor, and MJ dives after it into a pile of bodies. For an instant, he gets so tangled up in the arms and legs of other players that he can't tell for sure which limbs are his.

MJ comes out of the scrum empty-handed.

It's the Trojans who come away with possession of the ball, trailing 70–69 with just eighty-eight seconds remaining in OT.

Regaining his legs, MJ digs in on defense. He turns from angle to angle, depending on where the ball is, fronting his man and denying him the rock. MJ is determined—if a Trojan scores, it won't be the one that he's guarding.

But MJ is up so close on his man that he loses most of his peripheral vision. And Aaron Boyce takes advantage, setting a screen that MJ never sees coming.

Neither Malcolm nor any other Spartan calls out "on your left" to give MJ a heads-up.

As MJ gets bumped off his man, the Spartans are forced to switch around on defense, and MJ is left to guard Aaron.

The bigger player, Aaron immediately calls for the ball, backing MJ down beneath the basket. MJ doesn't have the size to block his shot. But his reflexes are much quicker, and when Aaron turns to shoot, MJ strips the ball away at his waist.

The rock sticks in MJ's hands, and a frustrated Aaron Boyce tries to rip it back, fouling MJ.

Troy has committed enough fouls in the second half and over-time combined to put Michigan State in the double bonus. So MJ heads to the foul line for a pair of free throws.

"You can put us up by three points in front of the whole bas-ketball world," Malcolm tells him. "This is your chance to live up to your name. I saw the real Michael Jordan in the stands before. Sink these free throws and even he'll know who you are."

"Don't worry, I'm going to bury this ball twice," says MJ. "Just watch me."

Standing alone at the line, MJ's entire body goes tight as the ref sends him the ball. He shakes his arms and shoulders loose, but that relaxed feeling doesn't stay with him the same way Mal-colm's words do about everyone watching.

MJ bounces the basketball three times in front of him, takes a deep breath, and then exhales. He brings it into his tense finger-tips, and raises up with his left elbow.

The second he lets the shot go, MJ senses that it's short. But even he's not prepared for it to hit absolutely nothing.

"Air ball! Air ball!" The catcalls rain down from the immense crowd.

MJ's teammates alongside the foul line all slap hands with him in support.

Then Malcolm steps in from behind, connects his fist to MJ's left arm, and fumes, "What, you only show some fight when you think you're standing up to me?"

NOVEMBER, FOUR MONTHS AGO

Even before he walked into his room in the athletes' dorm, MJ could hear the loud grunting from inside. It was Malcolm, in his usual spot on the floor, knocking out crunches with both of his legs raised high up in the air.

The pair hadn't asked to be together. They were assigned by the athletic department. It just worked out that way, with Malcolm arriving on campus and MJ's former roommate graduating.

"Malc, do me a big favor," said MJ, balancing a load of books in his arms as he closed the door behind him with his foot. "Take that workout down to the gym tonight. I've got a pair of exams to study for."

"I . . . don't do . . . favors," answered Malcolm, between deep breaths. "Big . . . or small . . . ninety-eight . . . ninety-nine . . . one hundred."

"It's not really a favor, man," said MJ, dropping the books on top of his desk. "That's just a figure of speech. It's more a common courtesy, something roommates and teammates do for each other."

"Is that right?"

"Yeah, and I might have said *friends*, too. But I haven't seen you contribute a whole lot to that equation."

"Hey, you got your way to act and I got mine," said Malcolm, popping up to his feet, before he wiped his bare chest with a towel and then pulled a tank top over his head. "I don't let any of my crap cross over onto you."

"It did today," countered MJ, as Malcolm began doing curls with a heavy weighted bar. "Ms. Helms called me. She was looking for *you*. Said you wouldn't pick up your cell for her. That you got a D on an exam in black history."

"Ms. Helms?" Malcolm said it like he'd never heard the name before.

"The academic advisor," MJ said. "She wanted to know if you needed a tutor."

Malcolm shook his head while counting off reps.

"I don't like tutors. They're too stuck up," Malcolm interrupted himself. "Besides, D is still passing."

"That's what I figured you'd say," said MJ. "So I told her I'd coach you up on it. I passed that class with a B-plus, same professor."

"What's the catch?" asked Malcolm, through the strain of the last few curls.

"No catch. It's for the team," replied MJ.

"That's good by me," said Malcolm.

"So how come you can accept a favor from me, but not the

other way around?" asked MJ. "Some magical Malcolm McBride *rule* I don't know about yet?"

Malcolm dropped the weighted bar across his unmade bed, with its shape making a deep impression into the mattress.

"It's not for *me*. It's for the *team*, right? Anyway, it's not a favor if it's your idea. Only if I ask you. That's the way it works," explained Malcolm, who started shadowboxing with himself in the mirror, which hung on the wall between a TV and a mini-fridge. "Why didn't you ever tell me you took that class?"

"Are you kidding me? I didn't even know you were in it," answered MJ, with Malcolm turning away from the mirror towards him, continuing his jabs and crosses. "I've never seen you with that textbook or heard you talk about any of your professors. And how can you get a D in black history? That's shameful."

"Nobody can grade me on that. I live black history every day. I'm even trying to change it by becoming another black millionaire, maybe a black *billionaire*," answered Malcolm, feinting punches to MJ's head and chest.

"That's not enough to pass a college class, to get credits," said MJ, standing toe-to-toe with Malcolm.

"Credits? I got street credits in black history. You know, that life experience stuff that can bury you if you don't pass," said Malcolm, bobbing and weaving with his head now, while still punching. "You wouldn't know about that, growing up in those soft Dearborn suburbs where everybody's got a front lawn with sunflowers."

"Well, I'm as black as you," snapped MJ. "And I'm the upperclassman here, so take it down to the gym."

"Yeah, but I carry this team. That cancels out that upper-classman shit right there," said Malcolm. "And you're not nearly as black as me. Remember, I went to *Martin Luther King* High School, and I live in the Brewster-*Douglass* Houses. The Douglass part gets its name from Frederick Douglass. He escaped being a slave and got himself an education. That's what I'm about to do when the NBA draft comes— escape being an NCAA basketball slave."

After one of Malcolm's jabs got too close, MJ said, "Stop it. I told you before, I don't like play fighting."

Teasing MJ, Malcolm popped him in the chest, with a force closer to a real punch than a tap.

On instinct, MJ punched back, hitting Malcolm hard on the right biceps—his fist slamming the tattooed portrait of Trisha.

"Hey, that's my sister! You don't touch her!" said Malcolm.

"It's not your sister. It's just a tat," MJ shot back. "You're the one who wanted to play this shit. Get over it!"

"Yo, just because you're not man enough to get a tat of your dead dad, don't lay your hands on my family," said Malcolm, before throwing a shove.

MJ tackled Malcolm on the spot. They went tumbling over MJ's bed, and then they crashed up against the wooden door, punching and kicking at each other.

LIVE RADIO BROADCAST OF THE GAME
7:32 P.M. (CT)

There are three broadcasters: a play-by-play man, a color commentator, and sideline reporter Rachel Adams.

Play-by-Play Man: An air ball from the foul line! My goodness! You know this young man, Michael Jordan, must be feeling the immense pressure of the moment for that to happen.

Color Commentator: That's why it was so important that he stepped away from the line just then, to shake everything loose, to reset and collect himself. That slapping hands with his teammates really serves a purpose beyond emotional support. It gets you to readjust your whole body, to relax yourself and come to the line again. And whatever Malcolm McBride came in to say, I'm sure it will help him to focus.

Play-by-Play Man: You've been to the Final Four and played nine seasons in the NBA. What's your mental outlook after an air ball on a stage this big? It has to be damaging.

Color Commentator: Personally, I haven't done something like that since junior high school. And I never did it in my college or pro career, thankfully. I have seen it at this level, though. It's tough to deal with. But I'm sure young MJ is no stranger to pressure.

Play-by-Play Man: All right, Michael Jordan readies himself at the line. It sends chills through me just to say his name, like part of me is reliving the past. Here's his second foul shot. It's up. It's perfect. Michigan State leads by two points.

Color Commentator: Great job by young MJ in blocking out the negative and putting that air ball behind him.

Play-by-Play Man: Roko Bacic bringing up the ball with sixty-eight seconds on the clock. The Spartans playing man-to-man defense. Bacic over the mid-court stripe. McBride in front of him. Bacic passes to Aaron Boyce. The last time Boyce was in the Superdome, he and his family were seeking shelter from Hurricane Katrina. But a different type of storm is brewing here tonight. Boyce passes down low to Crispin Rice. He puts the ball on the floor. Bacic cuts to the hoop. Shovel pass from Rice through heavy traffic. Bacic scores! He laid it in! Troy ties it up at seventy-one apiece.

Color Commentator: Credit the cut. Credit the pass. Like my mother always said, the best soup is made at home by more than one chef. And then it's shared at the table together. Terrific teamwork right there.

Play-by-Play Man: The crowd on its feet. Forty-five seconds remaining, McBride into the frontcourt with the ball. The freshman sent us into overtime with a last-second shot, saving the Spartans' season and extending his college career. Bacic cuts off McBride's dribble. The pass left to Baby Bear Wilkins. Now the ball right back into the hands of McBride. Michigan State with twenty seconds left on the shot clock, thirty-six remaining on the game clock. McBride trying to break down Bacic one-on-one. The Croatian glued to his every move. McBride into the lane. He hesitates, steps back. He goes up. He hits! He hit it! McBride made the shot! Michigan State is back up by a bucket with twenty-two ticks left!

Color Commentator: For all of his complaining about the state of college basketball, with that shot McBride says, "Put the NBA and all its riches on hold—I'm taking my team to the National Collegiate Championship Game."

Play-by-Play Man: Troy inbounds. Now they get it to Bacic. The Red Bull with a full head of steam. Seventeen seconds. McBride hounds him. He cuts right, McBride still with him. Now left. Bacic launches a jumper. It's good! It's good! We're all knotted up at seventy-three. Time out Michigan State, their last.

Color Commentator: Red Bull got the separation he was looking for. And without hesitation, he went straight up with the shot. That was beyond clutch. The only negative—he left twelve seconds on the clock, an eternity in this game. Now, can Michigan State and McBride answer back?

Play-by-Play Man: Before this current run in the tournament, Troy was best known for scoring the most points in a collegiate game. Back in 1992, Troy defeated DeVry 258 to 141. When the score was called into the *Atlanta Journal-Constitution*, the sports editor there thought it was a prank. That Troy squad didn't even make it to the tournament. Now here they are, two decades later, out of nowhere, threatening to win the whole thing.

Color Commentator: From what we've witnessed tonight, no one should refer to Troy as a Cinderella team anymore. Maybe entering this game there were still some doubts as to whether Troy really belonged. Maybe even some doubts in the minds of their own players. But this has turned from what could have been a fairy-tale, we're-just-glad-to-be-here scenario into a stone-cold war, the Trojan War. You can credit the man in the middle of the Troy huddle, coach Alvin Kennedy, with laying the foundation for that transformation. And everyone realizes that at the end of this tournament, the big-money offers will come flooding in from larger universities in need of a coach. We'll see if Troy can hold on to Kennedy.

Play-by-Play Man: So you think that in essence, this isn't the same Troy team that began the tournament nearly three weeks ago?

Color Commentator: That's right. Michigan State would have blown *that* Troy team out of the Superdome. These Trojans are the same in size and weight on the outside. But *inside*, they've grown immensely. They've bonded. I'd call it team chemistry, but that would be understating the process. It's been more like nuclear fusion.

Play-by-Play Man: And how does that affect Michigan State, the team with more raw talent?

Color Commentator: The Spartans have got to find that ability to grow within themselves right now. They've got to become something more than they already are. Whether that means someone besides Malcolm McBride steps up or McBride himself becomes the catalyst for making the people around him even better.

Play-by-Play Man: As the teams come back onto the court, let's go to our sideline reporter, Rachel Adams. Rachel, what can you share with us?

Rachel Adams: As everyone knows, Spartans coach Eddie Barker has been struggling with his voice this week. He had his team pulled in extra close around him as he feverishly diagramed a play. So it was hard for me to hear anything outside of that tight circle, especially over this crowd noise. But after the Spartans broke their huddle, Malcolm McBride looked at me and simply said, "Bank on it."

Play-by-Play Man: Here we go. Michigan State to inbound the ball. Bacic is all over McBride. The Spartans can't get it to him. The pass comes in to Baby Bear Wilkins instead. Now the Trojans double-team McBride, and Wilkins can't get it to him either. Nine seconds to go. Wilkins still holding the ball. Finally, he passes down low to Grizzly Bear Cousins, who's confronted by Crispin Rice. He sends it back outside to Wilkins. McBride still smothered by the defense. Five seconds. Now Wilkins loses the ball! It's rolling free. Three seconds. Two seconds. It's picked up by Michael Jordan near halfcourt. He heaves up a forty-footer at the buzzer. It's in! No, it's out! It's out! It rattled back out. Oh my! That shot was halfway down and it came back out!

Color Commentator: That could have changed young MJ's destiny. For a brief moment in time, he could have been more famous than the original Michael Jordan. But it wasn't meant to be.

Play-by-Play Man: Michael Jordan still sitting on the floor where he tumbled after that shot. Both of his palms pressed up against his temples, as if to ask, "How in the world did it ever come back out?" Here's the replay on our monitors. A desperation shot that should have had no chance at all. First, it goes in, and then rims out. Heartbreak City, folks.

Color Commentator: If you could see it on radio, and you're a Michigan State supporter, I'd tell you that this is what gut-wrenching looks like in slow motion.

Play-by-Play Man: We're headed to a second five-minute overtime session. And a fight breaks out on the court! It's between the two mascots! Unbelievable! Sparty and T-Roy—two guys in seven-foot foam rubber costumes—get into a shoving match in a wild scene that's now being broken up by security.

Color Commentator: This is what the Final Four is all about. Emotions pushed to the limits, and even more so now as we strap ourselves in for double overtime.

"When you go out there and do the things you're supposed to do, people view you as selfish."

—Wilt Chamberlain, who once scored 100 of his team's 169 points in an NBA game

CHAPTER NINE
MALCOLM McBRIDE

7:36 P.M. (CT)

Malcolm sees Roko extending a hand to MJ, reaching to pick him up off the court.

"Don't offer your damn hand to my man!" snarls Malcolm, rushing over. "Go worry about your own players. Go save your stupid mascot from catching a beating."

Roko holds both palms out in front of Malcolm, like a Trojan shield.

"No sweat," says Roko, backing away. "You can help him."

Then Malcolm reaches an arm out to MJ and says, "Next time pick your own ass up. Nobody helps you in this world but yourself. And you're not supposed to be hoisting bombs. You should be setting screens to get me open."

"Are you kidding me? I almost won it," MJ tells him, rising to his feet with Malcolm's help.

"That *almost* crap is for losers. I'm *going* to win us this game," says Malcolm, heading back towards the Michigan State bench alone.

At the Spartans' bench, Barker pulls Malcolm, MJ, and the rest of the players in around him.

"On offense, start by pounding the ball down low to our big men, Grizzly and Baby Bear," croaks Barker, looking almost directly into Malcolm's eyes. "Five minutes is a long time. We want to get that last foul on their center, Rice. They've got no one with any size to fill his shoes. So attack him. He's either got to foul or let us go to the hoop. Once they crumble inside, this game is over. Now, let's get it done."

Ringing inside of Malcolm's head is one contrary phrase: *Just get me the damn ball!* But of course, he doesn't say it out loud, not in front of Barker.

An instant before the huddle breaks, Malcolm is the last one to drop his hand on the pile, putting his at the very top.

AUGUST, ONE YEAR AND SEVEN MONTHS AGO

It was a few minutes past ten p.m. With his parents having just gone to bed, Malcolm grabbed the framed photo of his sister, the one of her full face smiling soft like a heavenly angel's, from the glass table in the living room. He snuck it out of the apartment and brought it with him to a house party in one of the other Brewster-Douglass buildings.

A basketball buddy of Malcolm's who was running the party—another guy going into his senior year of high school along with Malcolm—told him a scratcher would be there. Not just any scratcher, but one with some real skills. Malcolm had already seen the guy's work on somebody's arm—a blazing basketball being dunked through a hoop of fire, a tat that caught Malcolm's eye straight off.

At seventeen, Malcolm was too young for a legit tattoo parlor.

He could have asked his parents for a letter to bring with him. But Malcolm knew they weren't going to sign off on him getting inked.

A cousin of Malcolm's forged a letter like that once. But the artist at the tattoo parlor looked up his aunt and uncle's phone number and called them. So the cousin missed out on his tat and got himself an ass whipping at home besides.

When Malcolm first saw the scratcher at the party, he started to have serious doubts about letting that guy anywhere near him with a needle. The guy had a pair of silver rings through his nose and another pair piercing his upper lip. He wore a shiny purple shirt and a fedora hat turned off to the side. And he had an African name that Malcolm couldn't wrap his tongue around, even after hearing it twice.

But when the scratcher saw Trisha's photo, he said in a rock-solid voice, "She's beautiful. I remember seeing her before, around this neighborhood. I'm so sorry for your loss, my brother."

So Malcolm let him take the photo from his hand and go into the next room to sketch it.

"Don't stress what he looks like," Malcolm's buddy said on the down-low, beneath a steady stream of hip-hop. "That's how most of these artistic dudes are—way out there. What did you expect, for him to look like a baller carrying a big box of Crayolas?"

"I guess you're right," answered Malcolm, on the fringe of a living room full of dancing teens.

Then, maybe ten minutes later, the guy came back with a sketch of Trisha's face that was so lifelike it nearly stopped Malcolm's heart cold.

"How much for an ink of that here?" asked Malcolm, slapping at his right biceps.

The scratcher wanted $175.

That was fifty more than Malcolm had in his pocket, money he'd saved up a little at a time since Trisha's death. He'd collected that stack mostly by staying hungry over the last year, putting aside part of his school lunch money.

"Yo, Malc, my cut's twenty-five bucks of whatever tats get inked at my party. But I'm not about to make a profit off of Trisha's memory. Just slice that amount off right there and you're that much closer."

"That's cool," said Malcolm, connecting a closed fist to his friend's. "But I'm still short."

"Forget all the money talk," said the scratcher. "I'll take the one twenty-five."

"That's not a favor to nobody," Malcolm wanted to make clear.

"Favor? No, I'm being selfish. I'm doing this for me. It's for my art," said the scratcher. "Besides, I have a sister that's passed, too."

Malcolm took off his shirt. Then he sat at the kitchen table, which was covered with empty beer bottles and Doritos bags, while the guy made a carbon copy of his sketch. He pressed it onto Malcolm's arm, and it transferred over like a fifty-cent fake tat that you'd buy in a candy store.

The scratcher put on a pair of rubber gloves, and his machine with the needles started to buzz over the music from the party.

"Don't forget to breathe," he told Malcolm, with a few girls from the party hovering close by. "The people who pass out getting inked for the first time—it's not from the pain; it's because they forget to breathe."

"Man, I'm not going to faint," insisted Malcolm. "I never punked out like that in my whole life."

When the scratcher started, first Malcolm felt the vibration on his skin, and then the sting from the needle.

"This'll help," said his buddy, putting a bottle of beer into Malcolm's left hand.

People at the party kept coming into the kitchen to watch.

"That's her. That's exactly her."

"I feel like Trisha's here tonight."

It took the scratcher an hour to finish the ink, and Malcolm didn't look over at it once. Then, when it was done, he walked up to a plastic-framed mirror on the living room wall.

"It's like she's alive in my heart and on my arm now," said Malcolm, flexing his biceps to give Trisha's face even more expression.

Then the scratcher put on a big bandage over the tat and taped it down tight.

"What gives? Why you covering her up?" asked Malcolm.

"It's still a fresh wound," said the scratcher, handing Malcolm the name of an ointment to buy and rub on it every day for a week. "There are bacteria in the air. Believe me, you don't want to risk getting an infection. Keep it covered for a day or two."

On summer nights, Malcolm had to be home by midnight. But with his parents already asleep, he didn't stress over the clock. And he figured he was safe as he walked in the door fifteen minutes past his curfew.

Malcolm had just put the photo of Trisha back and was heading to bed when his mama came out of the bathroom in her robe.

"Did you just get ho— My Lord! What's that bandage on your arm? Did you get hurt? Stabbed? Did a doctor put that on?" she screamed loud enough to wake Malcolm's father, who came running out of the bedroom in his boxers.

"Calm down, Mama. Relax, I'm all right," pleaded Malcolm.

"Relax? You're hurt. I know you weren't playing ball this time of night. Now, was it a fight?" she demanded.

Malcolm's father rubbed his eyes, looked at the bandage, and said angrily, "I've got a bad feeling the only fight he lost was with his good judgment at a tattoo joint."

"Not a tattoo, Malcolm!" she hollered. "You're a minor! If some idiot drew on your skin, I'll sue his ass all the way to Toledo!"

"You don't understand, Mama!"

Malcolm's father ripped the bandage off.

That's when all of the yelling turned to silence.

His mama gently brushed the portrait of Trisha with her fingertips.

"I didn't want you to see it for another two days," said Malcolm. "Happy early birthday, Mama. It's a present for you."

She slipped her hand around Malcolm's neck, pulled him in close, and kissed him on the forehead.

From that morning's national newspaper:

PAYING THE PRICE OF AMATEURISM

NEW ORLEANS, La. — Attending the Final Four can be a costly endeavor—travel, hotel rooms and meals can put a severe strain on a family's budget. But as far as the NCAA is concerned, it is an appropriate burden for the families of players.

The parents, grandparents and siblings of players must pay their own way to attend the Final Four. The only perk the players receive are six free tickets to each game, which they can distribute to their family and friends, but under no circumstances sell for profit.

Perhaps this policy wouldn't come under such scrutiny by those who believe it's unfair if it weren't for the nearly 400 people who are having their Final Four trips paid for by the participating universities. These people include university presidents, trustees and their spouses, coaches' wives and children, several babysitters and selected booster (program supporters) guests who've made past monetary donations. In addition, a number of these people receive a $205 per diem for their trip to the Final Four, increased from the $165 per diem provided for the tournament's earlier rounds.

Why the difference in treatment between these pampered guests and the players' family members?

The NCAA views the freebie folks as "professionals," while the players are considered "amateurs" and are therefore unable to receive any financial benefit.

Though the NCAA admits the rules can be tough on players' families, they assert that it is necessary to ensure the integrity of amateur competition.

The parents of players have varying views on this issue.

"I think it's very wrong," said Maggie Davenport, a U.S. postal worker, whose son plays for the University of North Carolina. "As a family, we've had to make some really hard choices with our finances to see our son play. We'll have no new roof on our house this year. We'll deal with a leak or two and pray it rains less. Yet I know that some of those people getting a free ride here make 10 times as much as I do in salary. How is that fair? Without our children and the hard work we put into raising them, there wouldn't be an NCAA Basketball Tournament or a Final Four."

Television and marketing rights fees account for more than $700 million in revenues for the NCAA. Over 90% of that money ultimately goes to member schools.

Robert Cousins, a computer programmer whose son is a senior on the Michigan State team, has become more tolerant of the system over the years.

"At first, I felt it was hypocritical. Now I realize that if the rules weren't in place, there would probably be some parents taking advantage of the situation, receiving payments from all kinds of people, both good-hearted and bad," said Cousins. "This way there's never a cloud of suspicion. Yes, I've spent money on travel and hotels to see my son play, but I haven't had to pay a dime for his college education."

College boosters are also not allowed to give aid to players' families, not unless those boosters have a similar history of providing aid to the families of nonathletes as well. This way the athletes don't benefit by being on the team.

"I wish the NCAA could make allowances for

low-income families. After all, let's be honest, this is a business," said a parent who wished to remain anonymous. "Maybe years ago when the dollar figures were much less, a free college education was an equal trade-off. But nowadays, with the money the schools and the NCAA are making on the talents of our kids, it's a rip-off. They shine that light of being an amateur on you; meanwhile the professionals who run the behind-the-scenes of college basketball are in the dark somewhere counting their money."

"Love is the force that ignites the spirit and binds teams together."

—Phil Jackson (the Zen Master), who coached the Bulls
and Lakers to a combined eleven NBA titles

CHAPTER TEN
ROKO BACIC

7:38 P.M. (CT)

Roko can feel the body heat of his teammates as they huddle closely around Coach Kennedy. He's not sure if the splash of sweat he just felt on his shoulder is his own or someone else's. But it doesn't matter to him.

"Before we go back out there, I want you all to remember this. And I mean *all* of you, because even the guys on the bench have their part to play," says Kennedy, waving his hands like an orchestra conductor, punctuating the rhythm to his words. "No one ever knows for sure what they'll be called on to do. The longer this game goes on, the more we'll have to grow to meet some new challenge. We all want to win equally on this team. No one has any more of a desire than the next guy. So each of you, do your job. We all want to win, but we can't do it individually. That means we have to do it *together*."

As the horn sounds to signal the start of double overtime, Roko thrusts his arm forward, and a drumroll of hands slap down on top of his.

Then Roko says, "Together, on three. Ready—one, two, three."

"Together!"

As the players pair up around the center circle for another jump ball, Aaron Boyce says, "This time we're blowing the kisses to *our* girls."

Then Aaron blows small quick kisses at Grizzly, Baby Bear, and Malcolm.

"Nah, I don't think any of these dudes are my type," says Crispin, glaring into Grizzly's grill from a foot or two away in the middle of the circle.

Out on the perimeter, Malcolm jabs at Roko. "You Cinderellas better watch your kissy-face boy in the locker room, especially while you're changing."

"Why's that? He likes you. I like you, too—even more," says Roko, in a sarcastic tone. "I just don't want you to win."

September 15 (Grade 12)
My new high school teammates do not wish to play with me. They are mostly black players who maybe don't like the idea of playing with a Croatian. In the locker room today, in front of the whole team,

the senior captain Jared asked me, "What are you?" I answered him, "I'm a Croatian." Then he said back to me, "Oh, so you're a cartoon? Are you from Cartoonville?" Everyone laughed at me, and I tried my best to laugh along too. I will have to earn my way into their hearts with my basketball skills. I know that good passes for open layups can make friendships happen fast. Every day I will be the first one to practice and the last one to leave—a real gym rat—hungry for their cheese.

December 17 (Grade 12)
I scored 16 points today as the first player off our bench. The crowd inside our gym chanted "Ro-ko! Ro-ko!" as I hit two free throws in the final few seconds to give us a 63–59 victory. I tried not to smile too big as it reached my ears. *Always act like you've been there before.* More importantly, Coach played me for the final five minutes— Crunch Time (not Nestles Crunch). He had supreme trust in me and so did my teammates. They all slapped my hand and Captain Jared said I should go out with the starters to Burger King to celebrate. I thanked him for the invitation, but turned him down for a good reason.

After the game, and a shower, I had a date to get pizza with sexy Laura Coles. It was really her idea. She sits behind me in English, and today part of our writing work was to build our dream pizza. We both said pepperoni with green olives, not black. I can't say 100% that she didn't copy that answer from over my shoulder. But she said, "We should share a pie sometime." I jumped on that invitation without waiting, and asked her out for after the game. On the way home I kissed her for maybe a minute straight, with her mouth as wide open as mine. So I delivered at Crunch Time twice today.

I have more dates now with American girls than ones whose family come from Croatia. Some US girls even say I am Hot Euro Stuff!!! I am less homesick every day.

April 12 (Grade 12)
Today I visited Troy—the only college to offer me a scholarship to play basketball. I met Coach Alvin Kennedy, a black man. I liked him immediately. He studied about Croatia before meeting me. He said, "Bok"—which means hello in my language. He asked me if I would like to become a Trojan. I said yes and shook his hand on it. Then I politely asked why the team was named after a brand of condoms. Coach Kennedy laughed so hard that he almost fell down. He took me to the fountain in the main square of the campus and showed me the warrior statue of a Trojan. The statue had a

shield and armor, ready for battle. I thought that
Trojan's face looked a lot like Uncle Dražen. That
sealed the deal in my heart. Good-bye to the city
of Montgomery. Troy, Alabama—here I come.

April 14 (Grade 12)
I faxed my athletic letter of intent to Coach
Kennedy this morning. I am very pleased and
so are my parents. Now even my father thinks
basketball is not a waste of time because it will
pay for four years of college in the US (something
that is free in my country if your grades are high
enough). He praised the spirit of Uncle Dražen. "It
is a debt I will forever owe my younger brother,"
he said. I feel the same way. I owe Uncle Dražen so
much that I can never repay.

    I miss my mother and father in Croatia. But
I feel that I am not alone. I believe Uncle Dražen
is with me always. I feel him every time I touch a
basketball or pick up a pen to write my thoughts
in this journal. For my school newspaper, I just
finished an article on the bad food served in the
school's cafeteria—succotash (corn and lima
beans mixed together). I know that Uncle Dražen
would be very proud of me being a reporter. At
Troy it is possible to major in journalism. Maybe
someday I will interview the great Michael Jordan
and ask him how it feels to walk on air.

ON A CABLE SPORTS NETWORK PROVIDING LIVE
UPDATES FROM THE FINAL FOUR
7:39 P.M. (CT)

Announcer: As the Trojan War heads into a second overtime period at the Superdome, we have another encore presentation of Rachel Adams's interview series, *One-on-One*. This time, however, it's actually *One-on-Two*, as Rachel sits down with the two players most responsible for their teams' success tonight. Keep in mind that this segment was taped before the comments made yesterday by Malcolm McBride.

On screen, Malcolm McBride (left), Rachel Adams (center), and Roko Bacic (right) are sitting on stools, facing each other. In the background is a darkened gymnasium basketball court.

Rachel Adams: The two of you come from almost opposite ends of the world. Malcolm, you're from the projects of Detroit, and Roko, you're from Croatia, in what is essentially a postwar rebuilding period for that European nation. Both of you have experienced tragedy in your lives due to the violent loss of loved ones. Both of you have grown up to become incredible leaders on the basketball court. How much of your upbringing do we see on the court in your games? *(Her eyes shift to Malcolm)*

Malcolm: Every bit of it. I mean, who else am I? I learned to play in the streets. I learned to be somebody in the streets, all with a basketball in my hands. You want to walk down the sidewalk where I live and not have people mess with you? Then you better be somebody. Want to win on the courts so you don't have to sit out the next game? Want to even survive on the courts, not get shoved around? Be somebody. Because where I live, the courts and the streets are right next to each other. They're really the same, just a chain-link fence between them, and that won't stop anybody from getting to you.

Adams: Malcolm, how has losing your older sister, the innocent victim of a drug-related drive-by shooting, influenced that?

Malcolm: Trisha—she's my heart. That's why I keep her close *(tapping at his right biceps)*. She brings everything into focus for me, makes it all clearer. *(The camera focuses on her tattooed portrait)*

Adams: Roko, you lost your uncle, a Croatian journalist, in a horrific car bombing after he wrote a series of articles about organized crime in your country. He's the one who first taught you how to play basketball. Do we see the emotion of that tragedy in your game?

Roko: I hope not, because that was a very sad time for my family. For me, playing basketball is all about joy, to be happy and free. I keep the love for my uncle and his memory inside of me *(touching his chest)*. The war that's in my country today, an economic war of poor honest people trying to survive, has nothing to do with how I play basketball. Sport is our escape from all of that. The emotion I play with comes from my love of the game, the love for my teammates, and for my opponents.

Adams: So you have love for your opponents, Roko?

Roko: Of course I do. My first basketball opponent was my Uncle Dražen. We'd play hard against each other and then go home to dinner. We'd talk all night about what happened on the court between us. When you play, you want to test yourself and give your very best. You can't do that without an opponent also giving his best. So if you don't have love for your opponent, you can't have love for yourself. Your opponents make you a better person, a better player. That's how my uncle taught me, and I believe that it's right.

Adams: Malcolm, what do you think about that? Are you going to feel any love for the Troy Trojans this Saturday night at the Final Four?

Malcolm: *Love?* I can't stand them. They're wearing a different-color uniform than mine, and that's enough. They want to take from me what I want—a college championship and a higher NBA draft spot. All of that equals money. So I consider them to be thieves. The Superdome's going to be like my house on Saturday night, and I'm going to chase them out because they don't belong there.

Adams: Talk about the NBA, Malcolm. You've made it no secret that's where you're headed next year.

Malcolm: Can't wait to get there. It's been my dream for the longest . . . since I first picked up a ball. I don't know whose dream it is to play college ball. This is like the minor leagues. I'm beyond this. Tell LeBron and Kobe that I'm ready. I'll be joining them soon. And that if I get on a different team from them, to watch out for me. I'm going to be hell to deal with on the court—in commercials, too.

Adams: Roko, it was your dream to play college basketball, wasn't it?

Roko: Yes, first to play in high school, in Croatia, and then here in the U.S. After that, playing in college was my big dream. Coach Kennedy made that come true by offering me my only scholarship.

Malcolm: (*To Roko*) Man, that's all you got? One? I got offered something like a hundred seventy-five scholarships to play ball. How are you ever going to beat me at this game?

Roko: (*With subdued confidence*) My *team* is going to beat you, not me.

Adams: Roko, there's been talk among NBA scouts that through your play in this tournament, you've made yourself into a pro prospect. Will Roko Bacic be in the NBA one day?

Roko: It's a dream I don't let myself dream yet. I have a more important reality. I want to help bring a championship to my school, my coach, and my teammates. Something maybe nobody else in the country thought we could ever do.

Adams: I understand that you and your Trojan teammates have

written the number seventy on the heels of your sneakers for this tournament. Explain to us why.

Roko: Before the season started, Coach Kennedy told us about Katie Spotz, a girl from Ohio who crossed the Atlantic Ocean alone in a rowboat. It took her seventy days. *(On screen appears the image of a lean and blonde-haired Katie Spotz victoriously bringing her yellow rowboat ashore off the coast of South America)* She'd never done anything like it before. She even failed to get across a big lake in her one practice try. But she believed she could do it when nobody else did. That was like us believing we could make the NCAA Tournament, even though in the history of Troy basketball the school had made it there only one time before, and didn't win a game. So the day we made the tournament, we looked at the monthlong schedule from the beginning to the championship game. We figured that if Katie Spotz could make it seventy days alone in a rowboat, we could last those thirty days as a team. And we're still here.

Adams: And finally, I want to ask you both, what has the college experience been like? What's it like to juggle classes, practice, and the rigors of this tournament? Malcolm, you're a freshman. How is college different from high school?

Malcolm: College has been a lot like high school, only without the deans of discipline and school security breathing down my neck *(with a laugh)*. But seriously, I can't even say I really go to college now. Once the tournament starts, it's like you work in a basketball factory. It's your job to play. You're a pro without the paycheck. Right now basketball is my main job, not being a student. I've been living in hotel rooms on the road and practicing in gyms. I don't even remember any professors' names or what they teach.

Adams: All right, an honest answer. Roko, you're a junior, but it's your first time in the tournament. What has it been like for you?

Roko: Difficult. Malcolm is right—for the last few weeks I've felt like it's my job to play, like I am already a professional. But I keep up with my schoolwork also. I major in journalism. I want to be a reporter one day, so—

Malcolm: You know what? I'll let you interview me when I'm a pro legend.

Roko: That's very kind of you. I accept for the future. But you are already a legend—a legend of the mouth *(in a sharp tone)*.

Malcolm stares laser beams at Roko, who smiles slyly back.

Adams: *(Speaking to the camera)* As you can see, it's a very interesting dynamic between these two. We'll see what the future holds on the court Saturday night.

"Life is about growth. People are not perfect when they're twenty-one years old."

—Bill Walton, who won two NCAA basketball titles and three consecutive College Player of the Year Awards

CHAPTER ELEVEN
CRISPIN RICE

7:40 P.M. (CT)

The ref tosses up the ball. Crispin jumps with everything he has, but his legs are almost dead and Grizzly outleaps him by close to a foot, easily controlling the tap to one of his Spartan teammates.

Crispin tries to clear his mind. He knows the Spartans will be testing him, driving the ball in his direction, looking to get him out of the game with a fifth foul. He doesn't want to back off an inch on defense. But there are nearly five new minutes of overtime left on the clock. And if Crispin gets called for a foul now, his team will be handcuffed without a true center for too long of a stretch.

Malcolm immediately works the ball down low to Grizzly,

and Crispin confronts the big man. Since they're connected at the hip and waist, Crispin can feel the tenseness in Grizzly's body. He knows that Grizzly is getting ready to drive the rock right at him.

"Help defense! Help defense!" screams Coach Kennedy from the sideline.

But before an extra Trojan can get there, Grizzly makes his move.

Crispin backs off just enough to leave him with an open ten-footer. Grizzly takes the bait and settles for the jumper, putting all of the pressure on his own massive shoulders to make it.

When Grizzly's shot comes up short, the Trojans grab the rebound.

"Drive it at him, not jumpers!" screams Malcolm. "Think about what you're doing!"

Then Crispin sees Malcolm glare at Grizzly, rapping his knuckles at his temple, like the big man didn't have a brain in his head.

MARCH, THREE WEEKS AGO

Crispin took a deep breath and pulled up every ounce of courage he owned. His heart and his knuckles felt as heavy as lead when he knocked at that apartment door.

And when he did, the laughing from inside stopped.

Then, a few seconds later, a man's voice asked, "Yeah, who's there?"

"Delivery," answered Crispin flatly. "Flying Sushi."

"Flying what?" asked the man, before the lock turned with a loud click.

When the door opened, Crispin looked right past him.

His eyes caught a flash of blonde hair bolting off of the couch.

"Hope?" said Crispin.

"Excuse me!" the man fired back.

That's when Hope just froze.

Crispin watched her face tighten up like a stone statue. Then she took a stiff first step towards the door.

"John, this is Crispin, my fiancée—the one I told you all about," Hope said hurriedly, like she was trying to piece a jigsaw puzzle together on the fly.

Crispin stared down at the man with the curly dark hair, who looked like he was in his early thirties. He saw that the top button of his dress shirt was open and so were the buttons at the cuffs around each wrist. Then Crispin noticed a gold wedding band on his left hand. But that didn't ease any of the doubt in his mind. And after the introduction, the two never came close to shaking hands.

When Hope got to the doorway, Crispin never had a thought that they were going to hug or kiss.

"Anyway, what are you doing here, Crispin?" asked Hope.

"I was making a delivery when I heard your voice," he answered. "What are *you* doing here?"

"John's married to my second cousin, Iris," explained Hope. "They've been separated for a couple of months now. I've mentioned that to you before. So I came over to see how everything was going for him. We were just watching a movie on cable, a comedy."

Then Hope looked over at John.

He nodded his head to her story and then turned his eyes away from Crispin's.

Crispin worked hard to keep his expression blank, waiting to hear more. He saw that there were two bottles of club soda on the table between the big screen TV and the couch. That all the lights were on and all the window shades were open.

As the three of them stood in a triangle at the doorway, Crispin got the message loud and clear that neither Hope nor her *cousin's husband* was about to invite him inside.

But that was okay with Crispin. Because right then, he would have rather fallen three flights down into an empty elevator shaft than feel the floor beneath him inside of that apartment.

"You don't believe me," Hope replied to Crispin's silence. "You think something's going on here. That I'm cheating on you?"

"I didn't say that. You did," answered Crispin in a voice that cracked a little. "You told me you were going out with *friends* tonight, but *he's* the only other one here."

"You were absolutely right," Hope said to John. "Relationships *are* all about trust, not manipulation!"

"Manipulation? What manipulation?" asked Crispin.

He did not get a direct response.

"You were out here spying on me or something, weren't you?" asked Hope.

"No, I was making deliveries, trying to earn enough money to buy that diamond engagement ring you had to have," answered Crispin.

"It's always going to be about that now, isn't it? The money for the ring. You're going to make me resent even wearing it," Hope said, giving the door a little shove as she walked off, back into the apartment.

John followed after her, nodding in agreement.

Crispin stood there alone for a moment with the door still open a foot or two.

And after a few seconds, when he decided it was time to leave, Crispin reached for the knob and pulled the door shut.

Part of Crispin thought that Hope might come running after him. Only that didn't happen.

He walked down the three flights of stairs to get his legs solidly beneath him. Outside, Crispin unchained his moped and took off on it. He drove fast, feeling like he'd been shot out of a cannon without any nets for a safe landing.

As Crispin finally started to slow down and circle back around in the direction of the restaurant, he thought about the first time he'd really talked to Hope. It was almost five months ago, after a basketball practice in the Troy gym, and the cheerleaders were getting ready to practice next.

She was sitting alone at the end of the bleachers, tightening the laces of her sneakers.

In the two years she'd been on the cheerleading squad, Crispin had noticed her plenty of times. He liked the way her hair framed her face—like a gorgeous picture—and he could feel the energy jumping out of her body when she cheered. But he'd seen her around campus with other guys who looked to him like boyfriends. And she'd always worn a gold heart pendant hanging down around her neck.

As Crispin walked past the bleachers, Hope looked up and smiled. When he saw that the heart pendant was missing, Crispin finally made his move.

"Hey, your name's Hope, right?" he'd asked, sitting down on the floor at her feet, trying not to look so freakishly tall. "I figure you're an expert on the name, and I've got a question about it."

"About *my* name? Hope?" she said, making her back straighter. "All right, what is it?"

"Well, you know how in that story about Pandora's Box, the girl opens the box after she was told not to," Crispin said.

"Yeah, she lets all of those plagues loose on the world," Hope added.

"So how come the only thing left in the box was hope?" asked Crispin. "Hope's supposed to be something good. What was it ever doing inside of there in the first place?"

"Are you trying to compare me to all of those terrible things?" asked Hope, with a grin. "Because that wouldn't be very flattering."

"No. No. I was just thinking you might know the answer," said Crispin, with his eyes on hers. "I was thinking you might be as smart as you are beautiful."

When Hope blushed a little bit, Crispin felt like he'd won

something. He'd felt the same way when Hope accepted his proposal on the court, after he made that game-winning shot.

But that feeling had turned on him now, like the wind slapping him in the face as he headed back to Flying Sushi on his moped.

"Pressure can burst a pipe or pressure can make a diamond."

—Robert (Big Shot Rob) Horry, whose clutch late-game shooting helped win a combined seven NBA titles for three different teams

CHAPTER TWELVE
MICHAEL JORDAN

7:41 P.M. (CT)

MJ's heart is still pounding from his last-second heave rattling out of the basket at the end of the first overtime. He's breathing hard on defense as Troy moves the ball from man to man. Up on his toes, MJ dances around screens, reacting to the rhythmic *thpp* of each Trojan pass hitting its target.

Then, MJ hears the harsh slap of an open palm against the rock.

It was Malcolm deflecting a pass away.

The Spartans now have the ball, and MJ is on his horse, sprinting up court. Baby Bear whips the ball ahead to MJ, who spots Malcolm filling an open lane to the basket.

On one bounce, MJ delivers the rock into Malcolm's hands

before cutting to the hoop himself. Malcolm goes in for a layup, purposely angling his body at Crispin's, trying to draw a foul.

There's contact but no foul call by the ref.

Malcolm's driving shot doesn't go down, and MJ outfights his man for the rebound. He can hear Malcolm barking at the ref over that non-call.

MJ pump-fakes with the ball, getting his defender off his feet. He goes up for the easy put-back, but misses at point-blank range.

Playing as if his name was on the line, MJ rips the rock away from another Trojan and lays it up again. This time, the ball spins around and out, as if there was a see-through plastic cover over the rim.

Despite the echo of boos in his ears, MJ has more fight in him. He bats at the ball, desperately trying to keep it alive on the glass, until suddenly, off of MJ's fingertips, the ball hangs on the iron without any spin at all and then falls though the net.

MJ emerges from the crowd beneath the basket like a battered prizefighter who's just landed the punch of a lifetime. The Spartans now lead 75–73, with a little more than four minutes remaining in double overtime. And with those jeers having turned into a shower of applause, MJ heads back up court pumping his fist at Malcolm.

NOVEMBER, FOUR MONTHS AGO

As they wrestled on the floor, MJ got his hands free from Malcolm's and fired three or four clean punches into his grill. But there was no quit in Malcolm. He fought back like a wildcat, and his nails took a small patch of skin off of MJ's chin.

Other players in the athletes' dorm heard the ruckus.

They tried to come busting into the room. Only MJ and Malcolm were tangled up in front of the door, blocking it. And when Baby Bear lowered his shoulder to force it open, MJ saw a flash of white light as the door slammed into the side of his head.

A bunch of guys, including Baby Bear and Grizzly, separated MJ and Malcolm.

A senior on the football team sniped at Grizzly, "*Our* freshmen know their place. You let that McBride kid get away with thinking he's all that and a bag of chips. That's your fault for not setting his ass straight."

Grizzly exploded at Malcolm, shoving him backward at the shoulder with a stiff arm. "You hear the shit I have to take because of your attitude!"

Then Baby Bear stepped in between and said, "I feel you on this, Grizz. Believe me. But don't dent our scoring machine."

"Man, I belong to me, not any of you!" said Malcolm, pulling himself free of people's grasp. "I'll act the way I want!"

"Not in my face, you won't!" countered MJ. "I just proved that!"

"The two of you, shut up," warned Grizzly. "And nobody else here better breathe a word of this outside the dorm."

But out of spite, one of the football players had already called security, and within a few minutes, campus police arrived at Malcolm and MJ's door.

It was Sergeant Dixon, a five-foot-nothing black woman in her forties whose attitude was bigger than any other cop's on campus.

"Everybody back to your own rooms! Move! I won't tell you all again," Sergeant Dixon ordered. "I only want the two in the altercation to remain here!"

She had a pair of officers with her who were large enough to play football on the Michigan State offensive line. But she didn't need them.

"Nothing happened. I must have cut myself shaving," answered MJ to Sergeant Dixon's question about the mark on his chin. "I'm just no good at it."

"That's why we shouldn't give razors to children," replied Dixon without a stitch of humor.

After that, MJ wouldn't say another word. He just kept rubbing the growing knot on his right temple.

Malcolm wasn't in a talking mood either, especially with a swollen lower lip.

"I'm not sure what happened," Malcolm told Sergeant Dixon, raising the bottom of his shirt up to his mouth to dab the blood. "I must have walked into the damn door."

"Don't blaspheme in front of me," she demanded.

"Sorry, ma'am," said Malcolm, as if he was suddenly talking to his own mother.

"You expect me to believe it was the door?" she asked, with her penciled-in eyebrows raised.

"What did you think I was going to say?" added Malcolm. "I'm no snitch."

Sergeant Dixon was tight with Coach Barker. So instead of

writing up a report and filing it with the dean's office, she called Barker on his cell.

MJ could hear Barker's irate voice on the other end, and when that short conversation was over, Sergeant Dixon said, "Both of you boys are coming with me to the gymnasium."

The two walked on either side of her, and she did all of the talking.

"You can take that grim look off your face," Dixon told MJ. "Seeing the coach is better than seeing the dean. It's like the judge being your stepfather."

But MJ was concentrating more on Malcolm. He was jealous of the swagger the freshman was walking with.

Dixon escorted them as far as the gym door, and the pair entered on their own.

Barker was standing at the foul line beside a rack of basketballs, shooting free throws.

MJ and Malcolm silently took up places a few feet to his left. Barker drained a half-dozen shots in a row before taking his eyes off the rim to look at them.

"That's forty-nine straight," said Barker, picking another ball up off the rack and spinning it between his hands. "It doesn't matter that I've put on twenty pounds since my playing days. I never lost my shooting touch. How many do you two geniuses think you can make?"

Malcolm didn't give an answer, and neither did MJ.

"Well, if I miss this last free throw, I'm going to run those bleacher steps from the bottom to the top, ten times," said Barker.

The coach buried his final shot, barely jiggling the net.

"Hooray, no running for me," he said, barely cracking a smile. "Now it's your turn. Twenty-five shots apiece to equal my fifty. Add your scores up together. For every shot either one of you misses, you'll each run ten sets of steps. So I guess you'll be rooting for each other, if you're smart."

Malcolm stepped to the line first, and MJ watched as he sank all twenty-five, even with that busted lip.

Then it was MJ's turn.

He missed the first three shots, with Malcolm chasing down the ball for him, and scowling over every one.

"Don't worry about it, Mr. Jordan. I'm sure you'll find yourself a rhythm soon," said Barker. "That's what you search for in pressure situations—a rhythm or a flow."

MJ hit his next nine shots before the feeling left him again.

In the end, MJ made just fourteen out of twenty-five.

"Eleven misses. That's one hundred and ten sets of steps the two of you owe. But I guess that's better than being suspended two games for fighting. Better for you, better for the team, better for me," pronounced Barker. "Before you begin climbing, you boys want to tell me what brought this fight on?"

"He put his hands on my sister's tattoo," Malcolm blurted out quick.

"He said something I didn't like about me and my dad," said MJ with just as much gas.

Barker studied them for a few seconds, and then he said, "You two need more common ground. Maybe you should visit a junkyard together sometime. I'll give you each a sledgehammer and you can beat on abandoned cars, instead of each other. That's what you should both hate, right? Cars? Jordan's father was killed in a traffic accident, and Malcolm's sister in a drive-by."

MJ looked over at Malcolm, who was staring back at him.

Then MJ's right hand, which was hanging down at his side, suddenly balled up into a tight fist. Only it wasn't Malcolm who MJ was pissed at now.

"But you two *will* share common ground," demanded Barker. "You'll run those steps together, side by side. No leader. No follower. Now get moving."

It was five sections up, and five back down, with forty concrete steps in each section and the smell of stale sweat everywhere. After climbing the first couple of sections, MJ started singing to himself, trying to find a rhythm.

He tried a bunch of songs before eventually settling on something his mother always played on CD, Smokey Robinson's "Tears of a Clown."

It was a tune Malcolm knew well, one of his parents' favorites.

"Hey, American Idol, remember that song from the old Gatorade commercial? 'I Want to Be Like Mike'?" asked Malcolm. "Why don't you sing that one for a while?"

But MJ let that remark go.

Then, on their fifteenth set, MJ asked Malcolm, "You think Coach said that nasty crap about junkyards and cars so we'd hate on him and not each other?"

Barker was beneath one of the baskets, talking on his cell phone.

"I don't really care," answered Malcolm. "If he didn't have the keys to the NBA kingdom, I'd tell him to take all that sneaker company money he gets for the kicks we have to wear and run these damn steps himself."

Two sets of steps later, Malcolm said, "By the way, you should be saying thank you to me, benchwarmer."

"Why the hell is that?" asked MJ.

"If you'd gotten into a fight with anyone else, you'd have been suspended for sure," said Malcolm.

"Oh yeah?"

"That's right. I'm too valuable to lose. This team's not winning without me at the point."

"Wow, that's some favor *you* did for *me*," said MJ. "Thanks."

"I'm not a role model. . . . Just because I dunk a basketball doesn't mean I should raise your kids."

—Charles Barkley, Hall of Fame basketball player and TV analyst

CHAPTER THIRTEEN
MALCOLM McBRIDE

7:42 P.M. (CT)

"Force him left! Make him use his off-hand!" Malcolm hears an assistant coach screaming from the sideline, like a ventriloquist's dummy, with the near voiceless Coach Barker anchored at his shoulder.

Meanwhile, Malcolm's thinking, *Damn it, Coach. Don't scream it out loud for this Euro-boy to know, too.*

That's when Malcolm notices Roko adjust, fighting for more room to his right.

"Don't matter if you know what's coming," snaps Malcolm, as he cuts off Roko's dribble completely, forcing him to pass. "I could put you inside our huddle and give you the whole game plan. You'd still be a step behind me."

"I already know the game plan. Everyone does," Roko responds. "It's don't let Mr. One and Done stop us from playing like a team."

Malcolm follows Roko around a screen, sliding his feet on defense, and never crossing them, so he can move in any direction.

"Want to hear *our* game plan?" asks Roko, as Malcolm corners him. "Let McBride shoot the ball all he wants, do it all himself. Then we'll be playing five against one, in our favor."

"Except that five of you against me aren't enough," says Malcolm. "It's still not even close to being even."

With the shot clock winding down, Aaron Boyce takes a fallaway jumper in the lane. He misses, and Baby Bear gobbles up the rebound for the Spartans.

Malcolm gains control of the rock and starts up court.

Now it's Troy's turn to defend, with Michigan State leading by a bucket and less than four minutes to play.

"Come on and catch some of this one-man show," taunts Malcolm. "'Cause nobody can stop it."

"Bring it, son," mimics Roko from every movie he's ever seen about the hood, as he balances low to the ground with his arms spread wide.

"Oh, you're my daddy now?" Malcolm comes back. "Never gonna happen."

Malcolm fakes right, and then he crosses over to his left.

But he can't shake Roko, who's still right in front of him.

"Just me and you. Nobody else," says Roko. "You can't—"

There's a loud crunch as Baby Bear steps out of nowhere, knocking Roko flat with a hard screen.

Unguarded now, Malcolm takes a step back behind the three-point line. He turns the rock between his fingers, feeling for the grips. Then he lets the shot fly with his hands, falling into a perfect gooseneck over his head.

The shot goes in, and the ref raises both arms in the air to signal that it's a three.

"Red Bull-shit," crows Baby Bear at Roko, who's still on the floor.

Down by five points and with Roko dazed, Coach Kennedy calls for a Trojan time-out.

"Money McBride!" says Baby Bear, taking a running start at a powerful chest bump with Malcolm. "We're the new Shrek and Donkey."

"No, *he's* Donkey," says Malcolm, pointing at Roko. "But I'll take that Money tag."

From that morning's national newspaper:

MONEY BALL SHARED BY ALL BUT PLAYERS

NEW ORLEANS, La. — "Money ball" could easily become the new catchphrase for the Men's NCAA Basketball Tournament. And that dollar-green-colored basketball bounces in many directions, including the way of the NCAA, individual universities, coaches, television networks and companies that hope to rake in more than they spend in advertising and sponsorship. The money ball, however, doesn't get passed around into the hands of the players, without whom there would be no lucrative tournament.

Collegiate players rarely gripe publicly about the system. All of that changed yesterday when Michigan State freshman Malcolm McBride, who will leave after a single season of college ball to enter June's NBA draft, challenged it head-on.

"I heard that the NCAA makes something like $700 million on this tournament, and that my school could make 15 mil. I know part of that number's off my back, my sweat. That's like slavery," said McBride, at an NCAA-sponsored Final Four press conference.

How is a substantial portion of that tournament money generated?

The NCAA, which currently has a $6-billion 11-year TV deal with CBS, collects more than $700 million annually in broadcast fees and marketing rights. In turn, the network charges advertisers approximately $700,000 for a 30-second TV commercial during the Final Four. That price of advertising nearly doubles to around $1.3 million for the National Championship Game, with only the Super Bowl traditionally drawing more than the 40 million viewers expected to tune in. If those prices seem too high, network honchos can rest easy knowing that official NCAA sponsors are actually required to buy commercial time for the tournament.

The competing universities at this year's Final Four—Michigan State, Troy, Duke and North Carolina—are in line for a windfall of free advertising. It is estimated that during the course of the tournament, these schools will have each received more than $500 million worth of exposure. That exposure strengthens student enrollment and donations from boosters, and increases the quality of their incoming basketball recruits to field future tournament teams that could keep the money ball rolling their way for seasons to come.

Tournament advertising isn't limited to TV, Internet, radio and print ads. Some college coaches are now renting out space on their gameday sweaters. You'll see them prowling the sidelines with a sneaker company emblem or chain store logo emblazoned on their clothing. They also wear the sponsors' trademarks during TV interviews and to events. Many coaches, whose salaries already dwarf that of their university presidents, receive bonuses for advancing through various stages of the NCAA tournament as well. Several coaches reportedly have a bonus of up to $500,000 for winning the National Championship.

Video games licensed by the NCAA to outside companies mimic players' appearances and athletic moves. The games generate millions of dollars in sales without a penny going to the athletes. Because of their amateur status, college basketball players cannot endorse products for sponsors or even profit from the sale of replica jerseys with their name on the back. Yet players can be walking billboards for schools that sign exclusive product deals with sneaker and clothing companies. The players wear the shoes and other apparel during games while the school collects the money.

"Part of me feels like my school and coach sold my soul to some sneaker company. These aren't even the kicks I like to wear. They get paid for it, and I have to deal with the blisters on my feet," said a player at the Final Four who did not want his identity revealed. "I'm stuck in this system if I want to show the NBA what I've got. There's even a site on the Web that's reselling tickets for the Final Four at $3,300 apiece. But I'm not allowed to resell the tickets that my school gave me. Go figure."

Of course, every now and then the money ball takes an unexpected bounce. In 2009, Marcus Jordan, the son of Hall of Fame basketball legend Michael Jordan, began his college basketball career at the University of Central Florida. Upon recruiting Marcus Jordan, the university assured him that he could wear his father's Nike Air Jordan–brand sneakers, despite UCF's exclusive $3-million deal with Adidas for its players and coaches to wear the company's shoes and apparel.

"When I was being recruited, we talked about it," Marcus Jordan told the *Orlando Sentinel*. "They said they had talked to the Adidas people, and it wasn't going to be a problem. I think everybody understands how big of a deal it is for my family."

So for UCF's opening game, while the rest of the team wore Adidas, Marcus Jordan had on Air Jordans. He did, however, don a pair of black ankle braces with the Adidas logo. But that wasn't enough to soothe the sneaker maker, and Adidas canceled their deal with the university.

Seemingly lost in the fight for the money ball was the outcome of the game, which UCF won, defeating St. Leo 84–65.

"The time when there is no one there to feel sorry for you or to cheer for you is when a player is made."

—Tim Duncan, a Virgin Islander American, four-time NBA Champion, and three-time NBA Finals MVP

CHAPTER FOURTEEN
ROKO BACIC

7:43 P.M. (CT)

Lying on his back, Roko can see the crowd in the stands framing the faces of Crispin and Aaron, who are leaning in over him. All of the noise and voices sound muffled to him, like the Spartans had stuffed Roko's ears with cotton before they rang his bell. Roko doesn't remember the screen that knocked him flat. He just knows that his teammates have pulled him up to his feet, that there's a time-out on the floor, and that he's heading towards the sidelines.

Coach Kennedy is screaming at the ref over the hit that Roko took.

"That should be a flagrant foul! They tried to take his head off!" argues Kennedy.

Dazed, Roko looks up at the scoreboard.

He sees the Trojans trailing 78–73 with 3:18 left to play. And that hurts worse than any pounding in his head.

"Bull, are you all right?" asks Coach Kennedy, as Roko reaches the bench.

Roko tries to nod his head and the pounding intensifies.

So he holds his head and neck completely still, answering, "I'm good, Coach," as his teammates clear a spot for him and he sits down. "I'll shake it off."

A Trojan athletic trainer moves a finger from side to side in front of Roko's face, asking him to follow it with his eyes. And Roko does.

"Do you know what day it is?" the trainer asks him.

"Yeah, a day for comebacks," says Roko. "Now it's our turn."

The trainer gives Coach Kennedy a thumbs-up on Roko, so Kennedy begins to give his instructions to the team.

Roko tries to listen closely, but he has a hard time concentrating.

It's all a smattering of words: ". . . defensive stops . . . shots . . . keep moving the rock . . ." And over and over again he hears, "McBride . . . McBride . . . McBride."

Suddenly, Roko is fighting off a strong urge to vomit.

He works hard to give the impression that nothing is wrong, sipping water from a cup. When the team is ready to go back onto the court, Roko gets up from his seat. But now the Superdome is spinning all around him. The wooden floor seems to shift beneath his sneakers, and he drops down to one knee.

"I need a trainer here, fast!" Roko hears Kennedy's voice, before feeling the coach's steadying hand upon his shoulder.

May 23 (Grade 12)

I could not sleep well. I woke up very early this morning, before there was sun. It did not matter that it was Saturday. It did not matter that I could stay in bed as long as I wanted. I could find no rest in my mind and heart. The night before, I had no date, and passed on an invitation to a party with my teammates and friends. It was the first Friday night I stayed at home in a long time. I just did not want to celebrate anything. I wanted to be close to my family here—my aunt, uncle, and younger cousins. Today is the anniversary of Uncle Dražen's death.

It was one year ago that those monster mafia criminals in Croatia put a bomb into his car. They killed him for the dirty stolen money they wanted more of. The money and facts that Uncle Dražen's newspaper articles talked about. The anger builds up in me that no one has yet paid for this crime. I wish the movie heroes like X-Men were real. Then I could have the Wolverine chase them down like dogs.

Sometimes I scream out curses into the air or smothered into my pillow. I still cannot watch TV shows about crime families. I want to spit on the TV screen when I see old reruns of Tony Soprano's fat face.

I called my parents in Croatia. They were going
to church to light candles for Uncle Dražen's resting
soul in heaven. Only in the last few months has my
father put away his gun, thinking the threat on our
family is no more. I wish I could go to Uncle Dražen's
newspaper office and sit in the chair he once did.
But I can't. So I went to the Web and visited the
home page for his newspaper and read the front
page story about his memory. Then I went to
YouTube and watched highlights of old Michael
Jordan dunks. I remember how they made Uncle
Dražen and me smile. I held my basketball tight as
I watched. The same ball we played with in Croatia.
The same ball I took to the park to show Uncle
Dražen that I could dunk. I wish he could be here
to read my high school newspaper articles and to
see me graduate next month. I wish he could see
me play basketball at Troy next year. To see me
become a proud Trojan warrior on the basketball
court the way he was at being a newspaper
reporter.

Early this morning I took that basketball
and went to the park courts. It was too early for
anyone else to be there on a Saturday. I practiced
alone and went through all of the drills Uncle
Dražen taught me. I could almost feel him there
looking over my shoulder. I could almost hear

him saying, "More defense, Roko. Work harder on defense. It is the most important thing."

I was there alone for maybe a half hour when a boy nine or ten years old showed up with his mother and little sister. His mother took the sister over to the swings and the boy watched me playing from a bench near the court. Soon the boy came over and asked if he could shoot the basketball too. At first I said no. I told him that I needed to practice by myself. He kept watching me from the bench and every time I looked over at him he dropped his eyes down to his shoes. After a while, I felt like the Grinch who stole Christmas morning. So I told him to come over and play. I could see the joy in his eyes every time he let the ball fly at the rim. But his form was not good. Without even thinking about it I started to coach him. I changed the way he held the ball and the way it came off his fingers. Then I showed him how to dribble without looking down at the ball. He started to get better right away. Suddenly, I felt a spark in my heart. I felt like I was giving back a little bit of what Uncle Dražen shared with me.

Then the mother came over to ask if her son was bothering me. I shook my head and told her that we were just two players sharing the court. That made her son really smile wide. Maybe fifteen minutes later the mother called for the boy to go

home. I made sure he sank the last shot he took
for good luck. Then I gave him a high five before
he left. Later on, I realized that I didn't even
know that boy's name. But that is how friendship
happens on a basketball court. Names are not
important. Everyone is the same with a basketball
in their hands. All you can do is give to the other
players, on your team or the other team. All you
can do is your best, and that is giving. Playing
basketball with that boy this morning made me
feel better for the rest of the day. God bless
you, Uncle Dražen.

"You need a teaching coach who understands the game of basketball, not just some guy coming on the court talking about Xs and Os."

—Oscar Robertson, a two-time College Player of the Year
and the only player in NBA history to average double digits
in points, rebounds, and assists for an entire season

CHAPTER FIFTEEN
CRISPIN RICE

7:46 P.M. (CT)

With Roko on the bench, Crispin digs his heels hard into the floor, like the load he's been carrying is about to get even heavier.

"Stay in character. You can't wear somebody else's uniform," Coach Kennedy calls to his players from the sideline. "Just do your own job. We've got a lot of pieces to this team and they all fit. Let's put this puzzle back together."

Crispin takes a deep breath, trying to cement Kennedy's words into his mind.

The Trojans inbound the basketball, and with Roko out, forward Aaron Boyce helps the new point guard handle the rock.

Kennedy had called a set play during the time-out.

So the Trojans know exactly what they want to do on offense.

Crispin sets a screen along the baseline. Then Aaron cuts around him, freeing himself. But the ball doesn't swing fast enough from left to right, and the pass to Aaron is a full beat too slow, allowing the Spartan defender to catch back up.

Without Roko at the point, the Trojans need to find a new rhythm.

But while they're still trying to adjust, a pass sails off the court past Crispin's outstretched arms, and the Spartans take possession.

"We'll start our run with a stop on defense!" hollers Kennedy. "It's all about making this stop, and nothing else!"

Crispin watches Malcolm walk the ball up slowly. He understands that for Malcolm it's a game of cat and mouse against a new defender.

Then, nearing the top of the key, Malcolm flashes his speed, nearly exploding out of his shoes. He zips past his man and into the lane.

In a split second, Crispin makes the decision to challenge Malcolm's open layup.

He can't let his team fall behind by another basket.

Crispin plants his feet down an instant before Malcolm collides with him, knocking him over.

Malcolm's shot goes in, and the ref blows his whistle.

It could be Crispin's final foul, which would put Malcolm at the line for a free throw and a chance at a three-point play.

From the floor, Crispin sees the ref wind an arm back and then shoot it out in front of him, signaling Malcolm for a charging foul, *his* fourth of the game. A surge of adrenaline rushes through every part of Crispin's body as he bounces back up to his feet.

ON A CABLE SPORTS NETWORK PROVIDING LIVE UPDATES FROM THE FINAL FOUR 7:47 P.M. (CT)

Announcer: With barely two minutes remaining in double overtime, the Troy players are fighting for their Final Four lives in the Superdome, trailing Michigan State by five points. The big man in the Trojans' lineup, center Crispin Rice, has been walking a four-foul tightrope for several minutes now. Seconds ago, he was the beneficiary of a charging call. And just like that, Malcolm McBride picks up his fourth foul, joining Rice on that high wire. Recorded a few days ago, here's a glimpse at Crispin Rice in a more relaxed setting, without those perilous foul winds blowing. Our Rachel Adams goes one-on-two again, this time with Crispin Rice and his fiancée, Hope Daniels.

On screen, Rachel Adams (left), Hope Daniels (center), and Crispin Rice (right) are sitting on stools, facing each other. Crispin is wearing his Trojans jersey, and Hope is in her cheerleader outfit (a sleeveless red and white one-piece ending in a short frilly skirt that shows off Hope's shapely, athletic legs), and there is a good three feet in distance between their stools. In the background is a darkened gymnasium basketball court.

Rachel Adams: Well, not only is Troy the Cinderella team of the NCAA tournament, but they also have the Cinderella moment in college basketball this year. *(Cutting to the video of Crispin's game-winning basket and sideline marriage proposal to Hope)* So, here we are with essentially the First Couple of college sports, Crispin Rice and Hope Daniels. Hope, let me ask you, when Crispin started over to you that night nearly eight weeks ago, what did you think was going to happen?

Hope: I *(hesitating with her mouth open)* thought maybe he was running over to me for a hug or something to celebrate that basket. I never dreamed it was going to be a marriage proposal.

Adams: Did you have any indecision when he asked?

Hope: I didn't. The word *yes* popped out of my mouth before I could even think about it. Then everyone else standing right around us heard it. They all reacted and started cheering, before it had even sunk in for me *(scratching at the painted red T on her right cheek)*. A few seconds later, my brain caught up to everything. I said to myself, "Hey, I'm engaged. I better start to get excited, too." It was like being in a dream, and then thinking, *Oh yeah, this is real.*

Adams: Crispin, you've said before that this proposal wasn't planned. So I guess you didn't have the words ready either. Do you remember what you said when you asked Hope to marry you?

Crispin: I'll probably never forget it. I said, "That basket I just scored would mean nothing to me without you. You're my best friend. You're my life. Marry me."

Adams: That's so beautiful. Tell me more about what the reaction has been. I've heard that plenty of businesses want to help you get started as a couple.

Hope: *(Excitedly)* Some hotels have offered us free honeymoons. A wedding dress company called to say I could choose any dress they had, and a cruise line wanted to give us a trip.

Adams: I suppose there are some NCAA regulations governing what you might be able to accept because of Crispin's status as an amateur player.

Crispin: Just to make it clear, we haven't accepted anything.

Hope: We don't even have a wedding date yet. So if it's after Crispin's college career is over this year, it won't be an issue.

Adams: What about a diamond engagement ring? Has any jeweler offered that? Hope walked in here, and I thought, *She's not wearing a ring. I hope everything's all right with these two.*

Hope: They're expensive. Any jewelers out there, if you're listening, this finger's still bare *(holding up her left hand for the camera)*.

Crispin: *(Quickly)* But that's something we wouldn't accept from anyone else. It's my job to supply the ring *(taking a playful poke in the ribs from Hope, which Crispin doesn't smile over)*.

Adams: Now, as an athlete, Crispin is used to people cheering for him. But Hope, you've enjoyed a little bit of fame recently as well. It seems that since Crispin proposed to you, Troy hasn't lost a single game. And especially with this upcoming Final Four contest against the Spartans, the media has taken to calling you Hope of Troy, alluding to Helen of Troy from the Trojan War of Greek mythology. How are you enjoying that role?

Hope: It's been an incredible amount of fun. I'm very honored. Cheerleaders are supposed to be a source of pride for their team and school. So if people want to focus on me for some inspiration, it's great. And wouldn't every woman want a war fought over her *(with a huge grin)*? I think so.

Crispin: She's the queen of Troy, Alabama, right now. She can go anywhere she wants and do anything she wants.

Adams: But isn't it pressure, too, being the team's good luck charm couple?

Hope: Well, if we were going to have a fight, we wouldn't do it in public right now. We wouldn't want to jinx the team, or let down the school or city of Troy.

Crispin: Yeah, we'd have to do it in private. Too many people would be disappointed in us.

Adams: Now Crispin, you have a nickname, too, correct?

Crispin: My teammates call me Snap-Crackle-Pop.

Adams: Is that because your last name is Rice and your first name sounds like "Krispies," like the Rice Krispies cereal?

Crispin: I always thought it was because of my good shooting. That I could pop in shots anytime. But lately I don't know. I've been in a little bit of a shooting slump. Maybe I've been distracted by the engagement.

Adams: Tell me the quality about the other person you love the most. Hope, tell me about Crispin first.

Hope: Definitely trustworthiness. I've told him lots of times that for me it's the most important part of a relationship. And with Crispin, I have that trust in my life. I never doubt him.

Adams: Crispin, how about you?

Crispin: It's like her name—hope. That's what she brings into my life every day. There's the hope that things are always going to get better. And the hope I'll always be able to see things clearly with her in my life. It's all positive.

Adams: Win or lose come Saturday night, I'm sure that Hope and Crispin will have plenty to celebrate in the future. I know America wishes you both the best of luck in your lives.

"At least on the basketball court [growing up] I could find a community of sorts, with an inner life all its own."

—Barack Obama, the forty-fourth president of the United States

CHAPTER SIXTEEN
MICHAEL JORDAN

7:48 P.M. (CT)

MJ is shadowing his man on defense. Out of the corner of his eye, he checks the game clock. There's just 2:43 to go, with Michigan State still in front by five points. MJ is used to watching the final minutes of a big game from the Spartans' bench. He's used to seeing the backside of Coach Barker stalk the sidelines, not the front of him. And whenever his team had the lead, MJ would wish for the seconds to tick off faster. But now that MJ is on the court and contributing, he's in no hurry to push time ahead.

The Trojans are running a set play, and there is heavy traffic at the top of the key.

As a trio of Trojans crisscross, trying to lose their defenders behind multiple screens, MJ hears Malcolm holler, "Switch with me! Switch off!"

So instead of chasing his man through the stream of bodies, MJ stays put.

He picks up Malcolm's man moving towards him.

Then Malcolm switches onto MJ's man, running in his direction.

The defensive changes happen quick and seamlessly.

"Stay there for now!" Malcolm shouts.

"Got it!" counters MJ.

And suddenly, a part of MJ feels like he's been playing side by side with Malcolm all of his life.

The Spartans continue to blanket the Trojans, who can't find an open shot.

With the thirty-five-second shot clock winding down on them, the Trojans try to force the action. But the Spartans strip the ball away.

It's rolling loose.

MJ sees it heading out of bounds off of Baby Bear. He sprints after the rock, diving through the air for it as he reaches the sideline.

He tries to save the ball, but can't.

MJ goes flying into the opposing bench, with the Trojans' reserves, including a recuperating Red Bull, forced to scatter. He finds himself draped over one of their chairs, off balance, and almost sitting down in it. Then he grasps a teammate's hand, pulls himself up, and gets back onto the court as fast as he can.

NOVEMBER, FOUR MONTHS AGO

After MJ and Malcolm had run ninety-seven sets of steps side by side, Coach Barker gave them a little wave and a grin as he headed for the gym door.

"How many left?" Barker called to them over his shoulder.

"Thirteen," answered MJ between short panting breaths.

"Well, you boys keep on climbing. I'll see you both at practice tomorrow," said Barker. "And no more fighting. Like I tell you before every game we play, be the agitator, not the retaliator. There are always penalties for retaliation."

Less than a minute after Barker left, Malcolm told MJ, "I'd quit early, right here. But I know you're going to finish every last one. And I'm not about to let you say that you beat me at anything."

"How am I going to beat you?" asked MJ. "We're supposed to be running these steps together."

"Not anymore," said Malcolm, sprinting away and leaving MJ to finish the punishment on his own. "See ya! Wouldn't wanna be ya!"

MJ wouldn't chase after him, and just kept his own steady pace. Besides, Malcolm was wearing sweatpants, while MJ had on jeans that were getting heavy with sweat and chafing at both of his knees.

By the time MJ finished and got back to their dorm room, Malcolm was already stretched out on his bed watching the Cartoon Network, with an ice pack on his lower lip.

"I guess you got the workout you wanted tonight," said MJ, heading straight for his laptop and the pile of books on his desk without even changing his wet clothes. "I've still got exams to study for and a reaction paper to plan out."

"You know, I've heard that exercise opens up the studying part of your brain," said Malcolm, with any bad blood seemingly behind him. "Too bad you're busy with all of that. It would have been a good time for you to tutor me in black history."

"Yeah, that's what I'd want to do right now—tutor you," said MJ.

"What the hell is a reaction paper anyway?" asked Malcolm, hitting the mute button on the remote.

"Like that's really important to you," said MJ, flipping open the laptop and pressing the power button. "But if you have to know, it's a short paper, just a page or two. It's exactly what it sounds like: your reaction to something. I'm doing one on basketball for my sociology class."

"So what are you complaining about? That's no work," said Malcolm. "You write down how to dribble and shoot. Not that you'd really know how, especially foul shots. If you did, we wouldn't have had to run so many of those damn stairs. But you could ask me about it, and I'd tutor *you*."

"It's not about any of that," said MJ, still standing beside his desk. "I'm going to write how street ball is all social."

"Street ball is *social*?" mocked Malcolm. "Maybe in that pansy-ass Dearborn where you're from, where it's soft. Because with that thought in your head, I know you never played on the streets of Detroit."

"First of all, I didn't have it soft. I didn't even have a blood-father around to steer me straight on man-stuff, just a stepdad who was too busy with his own kids. And street ball's street ball no matter where you play. It's all about society. The players on the court practically create one of their own without a ref there. They make the rules, negotiate calls, choose sides. You should know that," said MJ. "President Obama grew up playing street ball. And he says flat out that it helped him to develop all kinds of social skills that he uses today."

"Yeah, where'd he grow up playing?" asked Malcolm, getting up to pull a tray of ice from the freezer in the mini-fridge.

"Hawaii."

"Are you serious? What was going to happen to him on the streets there? Was some tourist in a flowered shirt going to slap his ass with a pineapple? I should have known this was about you and Obama," said Malcolm. "I think you're in love with that brother, like you got some kind of man crush on him."

"What, I shouldn't look up to a black man who became president?" snapped MJ. "Who the hell should be my hero then? You?"

"How about the dude you're named after?" Malcolm shot back. "He's the greatest baller of all time. He's got mega-bucks, and his own sneaker brand."

"That kind of fame's not everything."

"Obama's not even the greatest president ever. His face isn't carved out in stone on that mountain, and his picture's not on any money," said Malcolm, flexing the ice tray until a row of cubes popped free.

"I hear enough about Jordan every day with this name. I don't need to think about him any more than that."

"I just think you're jealous because you can't live up to his skills," said Malcolm. "I think you should legally change your name to Barack Obama."

"And that would be easier for me?"

"Hey, I've seen enough of your game to know you've got a better chance of becoming president than the greatest basketball player that ever lived," answered Malcolm, putting more ice cubes into the pack.

"I'll just keep this name. I'm used to it now."

"If Michael Jordan was my name, I wouldn't complain about it."

"You wouldn't?"

"No, it would put everybody's eyes on me, and make me practice even harder."

"Not me," said MJ, finally sitting down at his desk and pulling a book from the middle of the pile.

"When I was fifteen, the cops nailed me for drinking beer on a street corner. I didn't have any ID. So when they asked my name, I tried to scramble for a fake one fast. I think Michael Jordan must have been on my brain, because I said something like Michael Jenkins or Michael Johnson," said Malcolm.

"Did you get away with it?" asked MJ, his eyes glued to the computer screen in front of him.

"Nah, they knew straight off. They made me write it down, along with my phone number and address, and I spelled 'Michael' wrong. I put the *e* before the *a*."

"That's brutal. No wonder you need a tutor."

"My pops was pissed when the cops told him I tried to use a fake name."

"Why?"

"He told me, 'Son, the only thing I have for sure to give you in this life is your name. I went and named you Malcolm for a reason, after Malcolm X. So don't throw it away, and don't disgrace it.'"

"I didn't know you were named after X," said MJ, turning to look at Malcolm.

"Well, I am," said Malcolm. "You know what you need, if you can't handle all of that Jordan jazz?"

"What's that?"

"A middle name to break it up," said Malcolm, surfing channels with the sound still off.

"I've already got one. It's Jeffrey."

"Then that's what you should call yourself—Michael Jeffrey Jordan," said Malcolm, before stretching himself out on his bed again, and pressing the ice bag back to his lower lip.

"There's only one problem," said MJ, behind a half-smile. "That's Michael Jordan's middle name, too. Like I told you, my father was his biggest fan."

LIVE RADIO BROADCAST OF THE GAME
7:49 P.M. (CT)

There are three broadcasters: a play-by-play man, a color commentator, and sideline reporter Rachel Adams.

Play-by-Play Man: A terrific attempt by Michigan State's Michael Jordan at trying to save that loose ball, diving into the Troy bench.

Color Commentator: It was just too far out of reach. But this young buck embodies the word *hustle*.

Play-by-Play Man: As Jordan's teammates help him back onto the court, let's quickly reset the particulars here in double overtime. The Spartans hold a five-point advantage, with two-eighteen remaining on the game clock. Trojans' possession. Just seven seconds left on the shot clock. At stake, a trip to the National Championship Game against either Duke or North Carolina on this floor two nights from now.

Color Commentator: And now at the mouth of the tunnel leading back to the locker rooms, you can see two different shades of blue as the players from both Duke and Carolina gather in separate corners, waiting for this contest to end. Their game should have started nearly twenty minutes ago, but it's been pushed back by the two overtimes. Yes, they want to witness who wins this

Trojan War. But I can guarantee you, they've been pacing their locker rooms like caged lions waiting to get out here. I know. As a player, I've been in that situation before.

Play-by-Play Man: The Trojans inbound the ball. Remember, they are without their floor general, Roko Bacic, who went to the bench after a devastating screen set by Baby Bear Wilkins. The shot clock now a nemesis for Troy. It's down to four seconds. A Trojan shot from the corner. It's off the mark. Michigan State has the ball and a chance to really stretch their lead.

Color Commentator: Troy isn't the same team on offense or defense without the Red Bull. If the Spartans score here, a seven- or eight-point deficit might be too much for the shorthanded Trojans to overcome.

Play-by-Play Man: The Michigan State fans are on their feet here in the Superdome. They're really bringing the noise. McBride on the dribble. He slips past his man. A fourteen-footer from the left side. It's off the rim, no good. Crispin Rice rebounds for the Trojans. That quiets the fans in green. We're down to a minute thirty-seven on the clock.

Color Commentator: Big-time players are supposed to make that kind of open shot, especially under these circumstances, to put a game like this out of reach. I've got plenty of respect for the political statement Malcolm McBride made yesterday. But I wonder if the weight of his words, along with all of that hype we heard from him about blowing Troy out of the building, has him thinking too much out there.

Play-by-Play Man: So you agree with some of his economic comments about the state of college basketball?

Color Commentator: I do. *(Clearing his throat with a small cough)* I just didn't think it was the proper forum to make them, taking the focus away from some of the players around him who worked their butts off to get here. But once it's out, you can't put the toothpaste back into the tube.

Play-by-Play Man: Troy advancing the basketball. They run the high pick-and-roll screen with Rice. He shoots. The ball rattles around the rim and falls home. The Trojans have cut the lead to three points, seventy-eight to seventy-five, with a minute and twelve to go! Let's get a quick update from our Rachel Adams, stationed courtside.

Rachel Adams: *(Speaking hurriedly)* Roko Bacic has been literally tugging at the coat sleeve of Alvin Kennedy on the Trojan bench, attempting to get himself back into the game. And he's been talking to his coach nonstop as Kennedy walks the sidelines. But the Troy coach has yet to budge, probably over concerns that Bacic could have a slight concussion.

Play-by-Play Man: Michigan State running some time off the clock. The ball moves from Cousins inside to Jordan outside, now

Jordan to McBride. Malcolm McBride takes his defender off the dribble. A running floater in the lane. Boyce a hand in McBride's face. McBride nailed it! He nailed it with Boyce hanging all over him! It's back to a five-point spread, eighty to seventy-five, Spartans on top!

Color Commentator: Clutch shot by McBride. Sometimes it's easy to forget he's just a year removed from high school, still waiting to turn nineteen. Of course, we wouldn't be in these overtimes if he didn't send us here with that incredible shot at the end of regulation. But that seems like ancient history now.

Play-by-Play Man: Ancient history, yes. That was nearly ten minutes of game clock ago. So much has happened since. Right now fifty-three seconds remain in double overtime. The Trojan faithful in red are imploring their team to score. Coach Kennedy is spinning his hand in a circle on the sideline, asking his team to play faster. The Red Bull is on his feet, too, behind Kennedy, cheering his teammates on.

Color Commentator: It's just superior defense by the Spartans without the threat of the Bull to break them down.

Play-by-Play Man: It's stifling the Trojan offense. Rice has to force up a shot. It's no good. Offensive rebound, Boyce. He puts it up and scores! The Trojans won't go away. They're within three points again at eighty to seventy-seven!

Color Commentator: Aaron Boyce has already defeated Hurricane Katrina here. So he should have no fear of the mighty Spartans.

Play-by-Play Man: Just thirty-eight seconds to play. The Spartans can run the thirty-five-second shot clock completely down, leaving Troy only three seconds to spare. Troy can't stop the clock.

Color Commentator: That's right. The Trojans used their timeout when the Bull got shaken up, trying to keep him on the court. But if the Spartans score, it could be over.

Play-by-Play Man: Coach Eddie Barker, who must have nearly no voice left at all, is pushing both palms down, telling his team to take it slow.

Color Commentator: The Spartans hold all of the cards at this point. They just need to execute.

Play-by-Play Man: McBride in a holding pattern with his dribble. The shot clock down to twelve seconds.

Color Commentator: Sometimes it's too stagnant with the ball just in the hands of McBride.

Play-by-Play Man: Seven seconds to shoot. Ten on the game clock. Now McBride makes his move. Several Trojans converge on him. McBride finally forced to kick the ball to a wide-open Wilkins from the elbow of the foul line. It doesn't go! Boyce rebounds for the Trojans. He dribbles out of the pack. Three seconds. Two seconds. Boyce lets it fly from just past half-court! Oh! It's good! It's good! Can you believe that? Aaron Boyce has just tied this game for Troy and sent us into a third overtime! Unbelievable! A portion of this Superdome is wild with exuberance! Another portion of it completely stunned!

Color Commentator: No matter what transpires in the remainder of this game, I think it's time for someone to say, "Instant classic!"

*"He who believes in nobody knows that
he himself is not to be trusted."*

—Red Auerbach, who coached the Boston Celtics
to nine NBA titles and drafted the first
African-American player into the league in 1950

CHAPTER SEVENTEEN
MALCOLM McBRIDE

7:53 P.M. (CT)

In the midst of Troy's wild celebration, with their players hugging each other and slapping hands, Malcolm won't walk off the court. His deflated teammates are already by their bench, waiting to huddle up around Coach Barker to prepare for an improbable third overtime.

"McBride!" bellows Grizzly.

"Malc, please, let's go!" begs Baby Bear.

Hearing their voices makes Malcolm's stance more solid, and the soles of his kicks grip tighter to the floor.

"Go where!" Malcolm shouts back. "I know where I need to be! Do any of you?"

Then he stares down his teammates from the middle of the court, like there isn't an ounce of real heart between them.

Barker raises a pair of fingers to his mouth, whistling sharply for Malcolm. When Malcolm doesn't budge, MJ takes a first step to go after him. But an intense glare from Barker freezes MJ in his tracks.

Then Barker walks out onto the court himself.

"Do our guys really want to win, Coach?" asks Malcolm, shifting his weight towards Barker. "I won this game for us twice already. Am I going to have to do it again? Against a team without their best player?"

The two usually act like magnets that repel each other. But at this intense moment their polarities somehow attract.

Barker puts a hand on Malcolm's lower back, escorting him towards their bench.

"That's why I recruited you," says Barker in a strained voice. "Because it burns inside of you to be somebody."

"No joke—better tell our guys to step it up," says Malcolm, increasing the speed of his stride and pulling away from his coach. "I can't do it *all* alone."

"That's right, you can't," affirms Barker, almost to himself. "Now when are you going to learn that?"

NOVEMBER, SIXTEEN MONTHS AGO

Malcolm rode the elevator downstairs with his father. Through the lobby's double glass doors, they saw Coach Barker's black Cadillac Escalade pull up to St. Antoine Street, in front of the Brewster-Douglass Houses. Then they walked outside together to the street to meet him.

Despite the chill in the air, there was a mob of a dozen dudes hanging out near the curb on the busy street, where a noisy sanitation truck was rolling forward maybe twenty yards up ahead. And when Barker stepped out of his ride, some of them recognized him right away from TV.

"Yo, it's Coach B!"

"Sign me up to play at State!"

"I bet he's here to recruit Malcolm!"

"I need me a scholarship, too. I can really ball!"

Barker had a few words for every one of them before he said, "Boys, you'll have to excuse me now. I need to spend some important time with the McBrides."

Malcolm's brow furrowed when Barker spoke to his father first.

"Mr. McBride, what a pleasure to meet you, sir. I'm Edward Barker, men's head basketball coach at Michigan State University, one of the finest institutions of higher learning in the country." He shook hands with Malcolm's father. "I'm here to speak to you about your son, and about securing his future."

Barker and Malcolm's father began to talk as Malcolm stood there watching them. The coach had been there for maybe two or three minutes and hadn't even looked in Malcolm's direction yet. And a stream of steamy breath seeped from Malcolm's partially opened mouth as his foot tapped at the concrete.

He'd heard that Barker was a baller in his day. That he was one of the toughest hard-nosed white players to ever come off the streets of Michigan. But if Malcolm had been holding a rock in his hands at that moment, he would have challenged that hotshot coach to a game of one-on-one as a real introduction.

Suddenly, Barker turned to Malcolm and said, "I've been looking forward to meeting you in person for a while now. I've seen the tapes of your game. You're one of the most talented young players anywhere. That's a fact. I want to see you wearing Spartan green next year, and leading Michigan State to another National Championship."

When he finally shook Barker's hand, Malcolm winced at the strength of his grip. And the coach took hold of Malcolm like he wasn't about to let go.

Before they all went upstairs, and with a few of the dudes hanging out on the street still tuned in, Barker turned back to Malcolm's father and asked, "Is this where the tragedy happened with your daughter?"

"About thirty feet away, over by that hydrant," Malcom's father answered.

"I have two daughters myself. I can't imagine what your family must have gone through," said Barker, bowing his head and making the sign of the cross. "Malcolm, I know about your tattoo. I respect that. I think it says a lot about who you are and what you value in life."

"Thanks," said Malcolm, who was wearing long sleeves and feeling a little bit like Barker had just nudged him off balance by bringing up something so personal.

"Coach, how did you know all of that stuff about us?" asked Malcolm.

"You see, I come here asking you to join our Michigan State athletic family," he answered. "It's only right that I should be willing to become part of yours, too."

Then the coach opened his wallet and pulled out a pair of fifty-dollar bills.

"I need you to do me a favor and watch my truck," Barker told the oldest looking of the dudes still hanging around. "Take this money and buy the rest of these boys some lunch on me."

Barker left to more cheers than Malcolm had ever heard for himself on that street. He was the seventh head coach to visit over the last month. But Barker was the only one to make that kind of impression.

Before they stepped inside the project building, Barker told Malcolm's father, "You know, that's an American car I drive. I understand you're employed in the auto industry. I'm an employee of the state of Michigan. I only buy American. I wouldn't think of costing us jobs by buying from the Germans or Japanese."

"I wish more people thought like you," said Malcolm's father.

Upstairs, the coach kissed Malcolm's mama on the cheek, and called her "ma'am." In the living room, surrounded by a worn-out floral-pattern couch and a brown leather recliner with cracked skin, Barker sighed as he picked up Trisha's photo off of the coffee table. He held it by the edges, careful not to leave any fingerprints on the glass.

A few minutes later, after Barker's first forkful of sweet potato pie, he said, "So what are your expectations from me and the university, Malcolm?"

"I want to play the point. I want to be the man, so I can be an NBA lottery pick after a year," said Malcolm.

"You've got it. You're my starting point guard, my top offensive weapon."

"That easy? No other coach is promising me that."

"Look, you're supposed to be the real deal. If you can't hack it on the court against big-time college competition, we'll both know."

"Believe me, I can hack anything," said Malcolm, crossing both his arms in front of himself.

"I know you can, especially with my coaching. I'm going to add to your game tremendously. I'll take you way past the next level."

"What about his education?" asked Malcolm's mama.

"He'll have to go to class if he's going to play, and he'll have to pass those classes," said Barker. "Then there's the second half of the year, the following semester. Even if you're intent on turning pro, you'll have to continue to go to class. If you don't, it won't hurt you. But it could hurt the program and your teammates if we lose future scholarships because you cause us to dip below academic standards."

"It's going to be that way at any school," said Malcolm. "That's the price of playing college ball."

"You can't put a price on an education, son," said Malcolm's mama. "Basketball isn't forever. I don't want you to be the dumbest smart kid anybody ever knew."

"Magic Johnson won a championship at MSU. He turned pro after two years of college and was the NBA's number-one draft pick. He owns a string of national movie theaters now, and a Starbucks in downtown East Lansing," said Barker, stirring his coffee with a spoon. "Plus, East Lansing is just ninety-three miles from Detroit. You can drive up to visit Malcolm in ninety minutes. That's peace of mind you won't get with an out-of-state school, especially those California colleges."

"You're not worried about his SAT scores?" asked Malcolm's father.

"Look, I'm not surprised the NCAA made him take the test again after his score jumped so much," said Barker. "He was red-flagged."

Malcolm had just missed the 820 he needed to be eligible to play on his first attempt at the SAT. Then he scored over 1200 on his next try.

"You mean he was black- or brown-flagged," said Malcolm's father with some bite. "Because no housing project kid could possibly make that new score without some kind of cheating. That's what they're trying to say."

"I understand your anger and the implications. But I don't run the NCAA. I work within their rules."

"I took the test again. I'm waiting for my new score," said Malcolm. "I know I did good."

"I'm sure you did *well*," said Barker. "That was you who took that second test, right? The proctor didn't think somebody else was you by accident?"

"I do things for myself," said Malcolm.

"He studied his ass off for it. I saw him with my own eyes," said Malcolm's father. "The first time he never studied a lick, like they were going to grade the test on his basketball skills."

"That's good enough for me," said Barker. "Now, do I have

your verbal commitment to play at Michigan State, to become a Spartan?"

"That's not binding, a verbal commitment," said Malcolm's mama, who'd put down her plate of pie to make the point. "I read that in the NCAA rules."

"You're correct. It's not. But I like to hear my recruits say it, that they want to come play for me."

"I'm leaning that way," said Malcolm, nodding in agreement with his parents.

"This family just has to make one promise to me," said Barker. "Plenty of people over the next year are going to want to be your new best friends. And the more success Malcolm has, the more they'll show up at your front door. They'll be agents, managers, and people who'll want to give you money, cars, maybe a rent-free house. Don't take a thing from any of them. It's all an investment on their part to get close to your son and gain a part of his future NBA income. If you take any illegal benefits, the NCAA could declare him ineligible to play in college. And that could put a big dent in his career, maybe cost him millions in the draft."

"Mr. Barker, my wife and I have lived in project buildings all of our lives, same for my son," said Malcolm's father. "But he's the one who's going to get himself out, through his own talents. We're not going to let anyone sabotage that for a gift, or the loan of a few dollars. Not in our lifetime."

"Being a part of success is more important than being personally indispensable."

—Pat Riley, a three-time NBA Coach of the Year who coached five teams to an NBA Championship

CHAPTER EIGHTEEN
ROKO BACIC

7:54 P.M. (CT)

Roko's thoughts are getting clearer. Now the only ringing inside his head is from the crowd noise and his teammates still celebrating Aaron's game-tying three-pointer at the buzzer.

Roko gets to his feet and puts an arm around Aaron's shoulder.

"How you feeling, Bull?" asks Coach Kennedy. "You got it together yet?"

"I'm ready, Coach," says Roko. "I'm like one of those terminators from the movies—the *good* kind. They can't kill me. I just get up again, keep on coming."

Kennedy's eyes find the trainer's. And without having to hear the question, the trainer responds to Kennedy's glance, saying, "I'm not comfortable with putting him back on the court right now."

Roko sighs heavily, but for the benefit of his teammates, he keeps a smile on his face.

"All right, same lineup on the court that ended overtime number two," says Kennedy. "Listen, it doesn't matter that we've never been here before. Neither have they. Not heading into triple overtime at the Final Four. Not against us. Now, all season long I've been preaching to you about Katie Spotz crossing the Atlantic in a rowboat. There was no way for her to prep for that. She just had to do it. One day she looked around and found herself out there alone in rough waters. So she had to deal with it and find a way to get through. But we're not alone. We have each other. Play like it. Keep rowing the boat together, Trojans. We're headed somewhere special. Maybe we can't see the destination yet, but it's in front of us. I promise you."

That's when Roko exclaims, "Row the boat—on three."

A percussion of hands slap down on top of his, one after another in quick succession.

"One, two, three," bellows Roko, an instant before his single voice is multiplied in number.

"Row the boat!"

ON A CABLE SPORTS NETWORK PROVIDING LIVE UPDATES FROM THE FINAL FOUR 7:55 P.M. (CT)

Announcer: They are underway in triple overtime at the Super-dome. Point guard Roko Bacic remains on the bench for Troy, shaken up and possibly injured in a collision. Undeterred, the Trojans, who tied this game in the last second of double overtime, grabbed the lead inside the opening minute of overtime number three. The Trojans won the jump ball, and on their first posses-sion, center Crispin Rice hit a fadeaway from about twelve feet. Then the Spartans' big man, Grizzly Bear Cousins, answered his counterpart with a basket of his own. It's currently eighty-two all. Both Rice and Malcolm McBride are playing with four fouls apiece. We'll keep the updates coming your way. But for now, from an interview taped yesterday morning, here's Rachel Adams with the coaches in tonight's epic contest.

On screen, Rachel Adams (left), Michigan State coach Eddie Barker (center), and Troy coach Alvin Kennedy (right) are sitting on stools, facing each other. Barker is wearing a green polo shirt with the Spar-tan logo on the right side of his chest and a Nike symbol on the left. Kennedy is wearing a red sport coat with a white shirt and red tie. In the background is a darkened gymnasium basketball court.

Rachel Adams: I'm here with a pair of coaches whose teams will square off against each other this weekend at the Final Four. One is a familiar face on the national scene, coach Eddie Barker of Michigan State. The other is new to making a run at an NCAA Championship, coach Alvin Kennedy of Troy. Gentlemen, welcome.

(Both speak almost simultaneously)
Eddie Barker: Thank you, Rachel.
Alvin Kennedy: Thank you.

Adams: You're both highly successful in your profession. When people hear the word *coach*, so many idealistic roles come to mind, whether it's respected teacher, guidance counselor, or substitute parent. Talk about how you view the role of being a coach in college basketball today *(turning her gaze towards Coach Barker)*.

Barker: *(In a raspy voice)* Coaching is certainly all of the things that you mentioned. Those are the staples of the business. But today, especially, coaching comes down to three basic things: setting goals, achieving those goals, and managing your time and your players' time efficiently so that the achievement part can happen. These aren't easy tasks for young people, but it's a reflection of the lives that most of them will live post-basketball, out in the workplace.

Kennedy: To me, above all, coaching is about communication. Coaches, players—everyone has to be on the same page and know what's expected of them. And that same communication has to carry over to players' lives, classes, and every facet of the extended family that our team becomes. Good communication stops the little negativities that naturally creep up every day, things like jealousy, anger, and misunderstanding. It stops them from becoming bigger things that damage the soul of your team.

Barker: *(Smiling in Kennedy's direction)* I'm glad you asked me first, Rachel. I wouldn't want to have to follow an answer that fine. That's why his team is where they are right now.

Adams: I think a lot of people would agree with that assessment. Of course, the coaching profession has taken a certain hit in the eyes of the public lately. I think the average salary for a coach with a team in the NCAA tournament this year is around eight hundred thousand dollars. And with the lure of even bigger money at more prestigious schools, we've recently seen a stream of coaches abandon their current contracts, universities, and players for more money elsewhere. Meanwhile, the players, many of whom chose a particular school because they wanted to play for that coach, are often left without the ability to freely transfer somewhere else. So the players, along with the fans, feel somewhat betrayed.

Barker: Well, it's all supply and demand *(clearing his throat)*, a matter of economics. Truthfully, that's the marketplace today. A winning coach and a winning basketball program can produce an enormous amount of money and exposure for a university. And a coach's first obligation is to his family and himself, to earn a good living, and make the money he can while he can. I know there is a certain moral obligation for a coach to fulfill his contract before moving on. But maybe competing schools should take the higher ground and not offer new deals to coaches already under contract somewhere else.

Adams: Coach Barker, you're among the highest-paid coaches in the country, aren't you?

Barker: I'm employed by a state school, so my salary is a matter of Michigan public record. But coaching is coaching. There needs to be a passion for it beyond money, because you didn't make that good living while you were learning your trade. You put those tools in place while you were still relatively poor. So it was passion that drove you, not a paycheck. That core love of the game is still the most important thing to me. The rest is just a satisfying gravy and stuffing at the Thanksgiving meal *(patting his slightly extended stomach with both hands)*.

Adams: Coach Kennedy, you are probably the hottest coaching property in the country at this moment. Rumor has it that major universities are ready to offer you four to five times what you're currently making at Troy. Coaching at a more prominent school would equal a larger shoe company contract for you as well. Your athletic director has said publicly that the university has no intention of losing you. That Troy will renegotiate your contract at the end of the NCAA Tournament. But they still might not be able to offer you the types of dollars you could see at a larger school. Has any of this been a distraction for you, your team, or your family? And what do you tell your players who will be returning next year but may not find you there?

Kennedy: Well, as far as my relationship with the players, we're busy concentrating on the task at hand. We're a family for right now, a close one, too. We're not going to let outside influences fracture what we have. We're all on different journeys and going different places in our lives. We understood that from the beginning. Players graduate and eventually coaches get replaced or move on. But we're sharing something special in the moment, so that's what we want to stay focused on. And it's not about *me*, because I wouldn't have the success without the players. It's about *us*, which includes everyone who puts on that Troy uniform. If the future holds other offers for me, I'll probably listen. But I'm not there yet, so it's not my top priority now. Helping this team to succeed is.

Adams: Michigan State has a confirmed "one and done" player in Malcolm McBride, Coach Barker. Has it been a difficult relationship with the superstar freshman?

Barker: I wouldn't say that. It's almost like dealing with a senior who has eyes for the professional ranks—only a senior usually has a little more maturity and feels closer to the program after giving you three years of sweat. But it's a business for those players. And hopefully, they'll take care of business on the court, because it's in their own best interests.

Adams: So motivation shouldn't be a problem.

Barker: Two games away from a National Championship, they shouldn't need me to motivate them. If they do, then something's wrong. I've told them all week, "There are over three hundred and forty division-one teams that would kill to be where you are right now."

Adams: Coach Kennedy, how do you like to motivate your players?

Kennedy: Well, I don't know that you can really predict what will motivate players. They're all different, with different personalities. Some need praise. Some you can challenge in public. Others need to be addressed privately. It's the same with coaches—we're all different, too. But as for me, I have a dozen individual relationships with my players. And when I'm talking to them all at once, I try to find that right balance, one that we can all relate to.

Adams: How about the tag "Cinderella," which has been attached to your team's accomplishments in this tournament?

Kennedy: Though my players may be too proud to admit it, I believe it's helped to take the pressure off. No one expects them to keep winning—no one but us.

Adams: Coach Barker, what's your take on this hoops fairy tale?

Barker: As a team, we don't buy any of that Cinderella nonsense. Those young men at Troy can play this game, and we take them very seriously. They're a worthy opponent.

Adams: So you're going to downplay being the favorite in this game with all of your team's size and strength?

Barker: The ball doesn't know that we're the favorite. It's not going to bounce our way because we walked onto the court with a bigger reputation or because our players have a few more inches. We're going to have to outwork them for it. I truly believe that.

Adams: So will your squad be intimidated in the least, Coach Kennedy?

Kennedy: I told my players before we arrived in New Orleans for the Final Four this week—it's a once-in-a-lifetime experience. You can smile and enjoy yourselves. But remember, we absolutely belong here. Don't look like tourists. We came to win.

Adams: I know that you two are opposing coaches, but under different circumstances, do you think you could be friends?

Kennedy: Basketball is an extended family. So besides the upcoming game, I don't think we'd have any obstacles between us. We were talking a little bit before this interview, and we both like to fish.

Barker: It's not lip service when I say that I respect this man *(shaking Kennedy's hand)*. I wish him all the best, just not on Saturday night. Maybe when this is all done I'll meet him at some fishing hole. But I still won't tell him or any other fisherman what kind of bait I'm using.

CHAPTER NINETEEN

CRISPIN RICE

7:56 P.M. (CT)

Crispin, sandwiched between a pair of rival Spartans, sprints towards the sidelines at full speed after a loose ball. His intense focus is split between the basketball and keeping his feet in bounds. The sideline is closing in fast, and everything surrounding the two pinpoints of his vision is a blur. The ball goes out of bounds off a green jersey, into the Trojans' cheering section. Crispin desperately throws on the brakes. His sneakers drum the floor beneath him—*bop, bop, bop*. Then the rock ricochets off the shoulder of a red cheerleading sweater and into the hands of Hope. Crispin straightens his body, fighting his momentum in order to come to a complete stop. The two are face-to-face now, with just a few feet separating them. The Superdome crowd erupts in applause for the pair. Then Hope takes a step back with the ball and loses her balance. As she's falling, Crispin reaches out and catches her.

The cheers grow even louder as Crispin pulls Hope to her feet.

"Thanks," says a flustered Hope, clutching the ball tightly to her chest.

Before Crispin can respond, a referee steps between them. He takes the basketball from Hope and then blows his whistle to resume play.

With the score knotted up 82–82 and everything in motion again around him, Crispin peeks back to see Hope being hoisted into the air by a guy on the pep squad.

MARCH, THREE WEEKS AGO

As soon as Crispin finished his deliveries for Flying Sushi, he went back to his room at the athletes' dorm on Troy's campus. His roommate, Aaron, was there with Roko, who lived in the dorm room next door.

The pair had taken a break from studying and were playing Crispin's Wii.

There were books spread out on Aaron's bed and on the floor of the cramped room, as the two stood in front of a TV, flicking the controllers tied to their wrists, tossing a virtual Frisbee to a tail-wagging dog for points.

"Hey, C-Rice, you okay?" asked Aaron, looking away from the screen. "You're all pale and sweaty, man. And I mean paler than usual."

"Yeah, I'm all right," answered Crispin, wiping the perspiration from his forehead with the back of his hand. "Just a rough day at work."

"You sure?" Roko followed up. "Because you look like you just ate some really bad sushi."

"Some customer stiff you out of a tip or shut the door on you again without paying?" asked Aaron.

"That stuff really happens?" asked Roko.

"Believe me, you don't know what you're going to get when you knock on somebody's door," answered Crispin, a second before his cell started playing "We Belong Together."

It was a text message from Hope.

Crispin sat down on the edge of his bed and read it to himself while Aaron celebrated his pooch scoring a perfect one hundred points for a leaping catch in the center of a bull's-eye.

?4U 1DR what you thought I was really doing there. Cheating? AYS? B/C AFAIR you're the one who proposed marriage. So you're supposed to have more faith in us. TMOT!

Crispin didn't reply.

"You know, I don't think I'll ever figure women out," Crispin said, deleting the text.

"It's all about communication, man, just like hoops," said Aaron.

"You think?" said Crispin, stuffing the phone down into his pants pocket.

"Headaches from your job and your girl on the same day.

What's that like?" asked Roko, loosening the controller from his wrist.

Crispin just shook his head and said, "Believe me, you don't want to know."

"Don't sweat it too much," said Aaron. "It'll probably all work itself out."

"I don't know. Maybe she's not the one for me," said Crispin, glancing up at the poster of *Sports Illustrated* swimsuit models on the wall next to his bed. "At least these girls never turn things back around on you."

"That's a big thing to say. You want to talk?" Roko probed again.

But Crispin's mind was somewhere else, and he never even heard the question.

Twenty minutes later, after Aaron had gone out for something to eat, Crispin was stretched out on his bed, staring at some world history notes.

Heading for the open door with his arms full of textbooks, Roko stopped and said, "Know what I like about you as a teammate? You've got your eyes open on the court all the time. I'm impressed by that."

"And how's that going to help me off the basketball court?" asked Crispin.

"Don't close your eyes to what you see, in you or anybody else."

"What do you mean exactly?"

"It's better to face stuff than pretend it's not happening."

"You sound like you know something here that I should," said Crispin.

"No, I'm not smarter than anybody about these things. I'm no James Bond double-oh-seven type with the ladies. But if you need to talk or anything, I'll be next door. I'm going steady with these books tonight," said Roko, before he turned the corner into the hallway.

The next morning, Crispin was waiting for Hope on the quad, in front of the fountain and the statue of the Trojan warrior.

He knew she'd pass that way for her nine o'clock class in advanced economics.

Hope was right on time, and she walked straight up to Crispin.

"Listen, I'm sorry about our arguing last night," she said in a low voice, looking around to see that no one else was within earshot. "I hardly slept at all. Let's just get past it. I was probably as much at fault as you."

"*Me?*" replied Crispin, with a bit more volume. "How do you think *any* of this was on me?"

"It takes two to argue," Hope answered. "It always does."

"So it was my fault for finding you in a strange apartment with a guy?" asked Crispin, appearing even taller as he shrugged his shoulders.

"You know something—you don't talk to me, you talk *at* me. That's why you don't hear," said Hope, pulling her books in tighter against her chest. "I already explained who he was. Just let it go."

"It's not that easy to forget—you alone with somebody else."

"That's so insulting," Hope countered quickly. "If that's who you think I am, why did you ask me to marry you? And why did you do it in front of the whole world? To trap me? So I couldn't have a chance to think about it? So I'd come off looking like a total bitch if I said no?"

"That wasn't it at all. It was about the moment," said Crispin. "Just tell the truth about that guy."

"All right, you want to know the truth," said Hope, stamping her heel on the concrete path. "Last night was really about your spying, about you not trusting me, and trying to control me. I'm your fiancée, not your property. How about a little room to breathe?"

"You need more room, you've got it," said Crispin, walking off.

"Thank you," said Hope, walking away in the opposite direction. "Because I deserve it."

> *"Sometimes a player's greatest challenge is coming to grips with his role on the team."*

—Scottie Pippin, a Hall of Famer who won six NBA Championships with the Chicago Bulls playing beside Michael Jordan

CHAPTER TWENTY
MICHAEL JORDAN

7:57 P.M. (CT)

MJ sees Malcolm turning the corner with the ball. So he steps out to set a screen against Aaron Boyce, who's guarding Malcolm. MJ times it just right, giving Aaron a real jolt on contact. Malcolm gets fouled driving to the basket by another Trojan. And once the play is stopped by a ref's whistle, Aaron confronts MJ.

"You guys like those bullshit little screens, don't you? You want to hurt somebody, right? That's why our point guard's on the bench," spouts Aaron, getting up into MJ's face. "You guys think you're thugs."

"We're just playing the game hard. The way it's supposed

to be played," MJ answers with just as much gas. "Maybe your squad's too soft for us."

That's when a handful of players from each side pull the arguing pair apart.

"If we were balling outside in the park, without these refs, I'd show you what tough is, little boy," adds Aaron, resisting his teammates' restraint. "I'd lay down the kind of rules you guys don't have the heart for. The kind of rules to make you go home early."

"I'll meet you there tomorrow," says MJ, with Malcolm giving him an approving slap on the rump. "No cameras. No refs. Nothing. Just you, me, and a rock. Any way you want to get down."

The two continue to exchange glares as Malcolm converts a pair of free throws and the Spartans take an 84–82 lead with 2:30 left to play.

Michael Jordan
Sociology Q205

Reaction Paper: Basketball Is Life!
(The Social Order of Street Ball)

Go anywhere that you'll find an iron hoop attached to a backboard. It could be in a crowded city park or a sweat-filled gymnasium. You probably won't have to stand around too long until you hear somebody say, "Basketball is life!"

The comparison is really not an overexaggeration, or the blind passion of some teenager who believes he is going to be a pro player and cash in on a multi-million-dollar contract one day.

Pickup or street basketball, which is almost always played without a coach or referee to enforce rules and regulations, is a social game that helps to build many of the qualities you need to excel in life.

How are those qualities developed in the players?

Because there is no power structure (coaches or refs), it is the players who build their own society and social order, establishing the rules, rewards, and punishments themselves on a 94-by-50-foot rectangular territory they've claimed.

Of course, if you're already part of one of these self-governing pickup basketball packs, you know what I'm talking about. You understand that I purposely choose the word *pack* because each park, gym, or ballyard across the country has its own pecking order of perceived winners and losers, somebodies and nobodies, and every caliber of player in between.

Whether you play half-court (one-on-one, two-on-two, three-on-three) or full-court (five-on-five), you also understand that basketball skills are only a part of what you need to improve your position in the pack. You'll need to hone other skills as well, including the ability to communicate and negotiate in a world where the sides can completely change every twenty minutes.

Here is just a partial list of the important skills you'll need to develop:

1. Choosing sides
2. Settling arguments
3. Bonding with strangers
4. Competing against friends
5. Accepting various roles on a team
6. Calling fouls
7. Honesty and values

If you asked me where I was born, I'd answer, in the city of Dearborn, Michigan. However, if you asked me where I grew up, I'd answer, on a Grindley Park basketball court. It was there I learned to be the person that I am.

I endured many trials during pickup games, and the accompanying lessons weren't always the easiest ones. But I made it, and I benefited greatly from the experience.

For example, what would you do if the basketball nicked off of your fingertips and went out of bounds, but no one else noticed but you?

Plenty of times I've stepped up and said, "That ball is off of me—it belongs to the other team." But did the players on the other team respect me enough to speak up and give my team possession when the ball nicked off of them? I can't say for sure, but I'd like to think that my honesty made a difference.

Of course, the players on my own team were really annoyed when my honesty once caused us to lose by a single point and we had to sit on the sidelines for close to an hour waiting to play again.

These types of situations come up all the time.

How about when a player purposely hits you with an elbow? When a player on the other team, or your team, cheats on every call or changes the score? When you're choosing sides, do you pick a better player over a close friend? When someone you barely know isn't pulling his weight or is taking too many bad shots, do you say something to him about it?

I'm proud to say that in my time as a pickup player I was able to negotiate all of these tough situations and grow from them.

But the pressure that comes with these situations isn't always easy. Players do fail at finding a place in this social order. I've witnessed hundreds of them run out of the park, and run off from the pack.

All of them weren't literally chased through the gates, though. Rather, they were shamed, ignored, or chastised into leaving. It was either that or accept their assigned roles as bottom-feeders—something they couldn't do.

What did those players who were run off really lose, if anything? It's a question that is nearly impossible to answer, because there is no way of measuring what they might have gained through success in street basketball. And what they might have applied that growing skill set to next—maybe the classroom, a career, relationships, or family.

Someone who did benefit from decoding the social order of street basketball is the forty-fourth president of the United States, Barack Obama, who grew up playing pickup games in Hawaii.

In his book *Dreams from My Father* (1995), President Obama credits his experience as a teenage pickup player with teaching him an "attitude" and "respect" that translated beyond the court.

Back then, the local players called him "Barry O'Bomber" because of the young left-hander's penchant for shooting long jumpers.

President Obama, who is viewed as one of our greatest public speakers, also learned about trash-talking on the courts. He learned that you could "talk stuff" to the opposition, but that you should "shut the hell up if you couldn't back it up."

That was probably a very good lesson for someone who is now commander in chief of the United States Armed Forces.

But even if you don't grow up to be president, participating in the social order of street ball can have a positive effect on you. Perhaps at this very moment, a future policeman is calling a foul on another pickup player. Or a future teacher is explaining to somebody why his or her move was a traveling violation. Or someone destined to become a judge is negotiating a dispute between two rival players who see the same action on the court differently.

As for myself, I hope to one day become a broadcaster. Basketball has a huge oral tradition, whether it is describing incredible moves, trash-talking, or communicating with other players on the court. I know that the language skills I've sharpened through years of playing street ball and participating in its society will serve me well in achieving my broadcasting dream.

*"There is nothing wrong with dedication and goals,
but if you focus on yourself, all the lights fade away
and you become a fleeting moment in life."*

—"Pistol Pete" Maravich, college basketball's all-time
leading scorer, who averaged 44.2 points per game

CHAPTER TWENTY-ONE
MALCOLM McBRIDE

7:58 P.M. (CT)

On defense, Malcolm is hounding the Trojans' substitute point guard, harassing him as he tries to advance the ball over half-court.

"You can't deal with this kind of heat," says Malcolm, chasing him into a corner. "I know you want to be back on that bench, not out here with me."

Malcolm can read the frustration in his opponent's eyes, and he knows a pass is coming, just to escape all of the pressure.

A fraction of a second before the ball leaves the opposing point guard's hands, Malcolm leaps into a passing lane to intercept it. His anticipation is perfect. But Malcolm's legs are already in high gear, streaking towards the opposite hoop before he even secures the ball. And Malcolm fumbles it away out of bounds.

After a few more strides, he punches his open left hand with his right fist in response.

Then Malcolm scolds the hand, as if it were a teammate who'd let him down.

"That was going to be steal number seven tonight, my most in any game. You really blew that shit," he snaps at it.

Walking back into position to defend the point guard, Malcolm tells him, "Don't worry, another steal's coming. I can feel it."

Within the next twenty seconds of game clock, Malcolm steps in front of a crosscourt pass intended for a Trojan. He makes the steal and bolts for the basket at the far end of the court. Up ahead of him is a wide-open Baby Bear Wilkins asking for the ball. But Malcolm keeps possession of the rock, rocketing past Baby Bear to score on the breakaway layup.

"Sorry, Double B, I just wanted to make sure it got done," says Malcolm.

"So long as we beat these guys, Malc," says Baby Bear. "That's all I care about."

The basket gives the Spartans an 86–82 lead with 1:55 remaining in triple overtime. And in Malcolm's mind, he knows that bucket represents his thirty-second and thirty-third points of the game.

NOVEMBER, SIXTEEN MONTHS AGO

A few weeks after giving his verbal commitment to play for Coach Barker, Malcolm and his father went to Elmwood Cemetery to visit Trisha's grave. It wasn't something they had planned. It was Saturday on Thanksgiving weekend, Malcolm's senior year of high school, and his mother had taken the car to go shopping with her sister.

"Son, I feel like going to see Trisha this morning," said Malcolm's father, looking out of their living room window. "It's starting to snow outside, first of the season. Your sister loved to play in the snow when she was little. You both did. Made me pull the two of you around on that Flexible Flyer for hours, like I was some kind of workhorse. So it's got me thinking about her. You want to tag along?"

"Sure, Pop, I'll go. Give her the news about my scholarship in person," answered Malcolm, turning off the TV, before he grabbed his good corduroy coat from the hall closet.

Malcolm and his father rode the city bus to Elmwood.

It let them off in front of the cemetery's big iron gates, and just outside, Malcolm's father bought a small wreath of flowers to take to Trisha.

There was hardly any wind. The snow fell straight down in big soft flakes that settled on their heads and shoulders.

"It's this way, past that pair of oak trees," said Malcolm, veering to the left, off of the paved path, and heading up a small hill.

Malcolm remembered from the last time he'd been there, with his parents about a month ago.

"I know where she is," said his father, trailing a step or two behind. "I could find her grave in my sleep if I had to."

But within a few moments, Malcolm and his father had walked nearly twenty yards too far, searching for the small gray headstone with Trisha's name cut into it.

They both stopped in their tracks at the same time, looking at each other, and then at the headstones around them.

Malcolm's father said, "Must be this frosting on the ground that's got us confused. I can't—"

"No, Pop, look there," interrupted Malcolm, with his brown eyes opened as wide as they could be.

Trisha's simple stone had been replaced by the biggest, most impressive one Malcolm and his father could see anywhere around them.

"Beloved daughter. Beloved sister," Malcolm read out loud as the two of them moved closer to it.

There were two angels on top, blowing horns, and a girl playing the snare drum carved into the granite monument.

"Did you and Mom do this?" asked Malcolm. But as soon as he asked, he knew it didn't make any sense. His parents had barely had enough money to pay for Trisha's funeral and the original headstone.

"You'd have been the first to know," his father said, shaking his head in disbelief.

"Where do you think it came from, then?" asked Malcolm, pulling his gloves off to feel the polished stone with his bare fingers.

"I have no idea in this world," answered his father, who brushed away the snow from the base of the headstone to lay the flowered wreath there.

"So somebody just took the old one away without telling us?" said Malcolm. "That's crazy. Stuff like that just doesn't happen, does it, Pop?"

"Not without somebody paying for it. And this headstone looks like it cost a bundle."

Malcolm thought about what Coach Barker had said, about people wanting to buy things for him.

"You think it's about basketball, about me going pro soon? Maybe somebody wants something in return?"

"I wouldn't say that out loud again for no reason, son."

"So you think it is?" Malcolm asked.

The coach had specifically told him not to take anything from anyone. But how could he return a headstone?

Malcolm's father didn't answer. He just brushed the now rapidly falling snow from his shoulders.

"What are we going to do?" Malcolm asked.

"I don't truthfully know. But with God as my witness, if there's one thing I'd hate more than seeing my baby's grave disturbed, it would be seeing it done twice. So I'm not going to ask to have it removed. And I want to put one thing into your mind, son."

"What's that, Pop?"

"No matter who did it, this couldn't be a gift to *you*. It's to your sister. And she's gone to heaven now."

Malcolm nodded his head.

"There has to be an explanation. But it's not on us to track down what it is. I don't want to find out your sister's memory is being manipulated. I don't think your mama could live with the rage it would cause her. So let me be the one to tell her about this. We'll put our faith in God for now, that this was done for the right reasons. We'll keep it quiet and respectful."

"I'm solid with you on all of that, Pop," said Malcolm, taking his fingertips from the stone. "I won't talk about it to nobody. I promise."

"For a long time, I operated under the Chinese proverb that there are four kinds of leaders: those who you laugh at, those who you hate, those who you love, and those who you don't even know that they're leaders."

—Bill Bradley, a Rhodes Scholar and two-time NBA Champion who was later elected to the U.S. Senate

CHAPTER TWENTY-TWO
ROKO BACIC

7:59 P.M. (CT)

With the game clock having run down inside of two minutes and the Trojans trailing by four points, Roko tugs at the back of Coach Kennedy's suit jacket from his seat on the bench.

"Get me back into the game, Coach. I'm fine now," pleads Roko.

Kennedy pulls away from him and paces the sideline.

"Prove it to me, Bull. Prove your head's clear," says Kennedy. "Give me a four."

"Four. *Rocky IV*, with the Russian boxer. *Shrek Forever After*," says Roko. "*Live Free or Die Hard. Star Wars: Episode IV—A New Hope.*"

"A three," says Kennedy, turning to look directly into Roko's eyes.

"*Terminator 3: Rise of the Machines. The Matrix Revolutions. The Bourne Ultimatum. Spider-Man 3*, with the Sandman and black-costumed web-slinger."

"A two," says Kennedy, bringing his face closer to Roko's.

"*The Mummy Returns. Indiana Jones and the Temple of Doom. Hellboy II: The Golden Army. 2 Fast 2 Furious. Tomb Raider: The Cradle of Life.*"

"Is it completely out of the question?" Kennedy asks the trainer, who's sitting next to Roko.

"I'm satisfied he's thinking straighter," responds the trainer. "It's your call, Coach."

"All right. Get—"

Roko springs off the bench before Kennedy can finish his words.

The crowd roars and the players on the court take notice.

"Get back on the point and run the show for us," says Kennedy, following Roko to the scorer's table. "Give us that surge we need."

"I'll give you everything I've got, Coach," says Roko, kneeling in front of the scorer's table, ready to check in.

And as he prepares himself mentally to reenter the game, out of the corner of his eye, Roko glimpses Hope kicking her legs up high, cheering the Trojans on.

February 24 (five weeks ago)

Tonight, I believe that Hope came on to me. I am almost totally convinced. We were at a crowded party in an apartment just a block off campus. It was before Crispin got there, while he was still finishing his deliveries. I had this strange feeling in my bones that Hope was smiling too much at me. At first, I thought it might all be my imagination. But then she came up to me and said close to my ear, "You know, I've always liked red hair. I think it's really cute on a guy."

"Thank you," I told her. Then I excused myself to the bathroom. That was probably best, because I had no other response, except maybe to say, "I'm a playa hater. Not a playa."

I know she had at least two beers, so maybe it was the Budweiser talking. Then, shortly after Crispin arrived, I left.

As I walked home, I was completely torn between two different things—between friendship for Crispin and the idea of minding my own business. I understand that sometimes girls like to play stupid games to make their boyfriends jealous. And it's probably worse with a fiancée. I was also worried that telling Crispin could put a huge obstacle between us, hurting our chemistry on the court. And if I was wrong about her flirting, I would have looked like a total idiot—"Jackass 3D."

Then the idea came to me to call Coach Kennedy for advice. I used his emergency cell number and got him at home. I explained the whole messy situation, and he told me that I did the correct thing. "I'm glad you called me with this," said Coach. "Put the entire incident out of your mind, like it never happened. And don't approach Crispin with any details. I've noticed how uptight he's been lately. When the time is right, I'll speak to him myself about the pressures of being engaged."

So that's where I've left the problem for now, with Coach Kennedy, hoping for the best solution.

LIVE RADIO BROADCAST OF THE GAME
7:59 P.M. (CT)

There are three broadcasters: a play-by-play man, a color commentator, and sideline reporter Rachel Adams.

Play-by-Play Man: Listen to this Superdome crowd roar as the Red Bull, Roko Bacic, pops up off the Trojans' bench.

Color Commentator: The kid from Croatia is all heart. He gives so much of himself. That's why he's so popular. But above all, this is a war and you need your warriors, your leaders. He'd have to be unconscious not to finish this contest.

Play-by-Play Man: And on the court, a smart play by Troy's Aaron Boyce to send the ball out of bounds off a Spartan's leg. That stops the clock with a minute forty-two remaining and allows Bacic to enter the game.

Color Commentator: That's a high basketball IQ right there with Boyce.

Play-by-Play Man: Let's get a report from Rachel Adams.

Rachel Adams: I could tell two things from behind the Trojans' bench: that Roko Bacic wanted back into this game badly, and that coach Alvin Kennedy agonized over the decision to return his shaken point guard to action. But after a short conversation in which Kennedy seemed to be quizzing Bacic, trying to assess whether the cobwebs in his head had indeed cleared, the Red Bull is once again at the Trojans' helm.

Play-by-Play Man: Bacic with the ball in his hands immediately. He's on the dribble. A beautiful crossover move. And just like that he takes the ball at Malcolm McBride and scores on a driving layup. The Michigan State lead is cut to two points with ninety seconds left on the clock.

Color Commentator: McBride, with four fouls, played him soft, and the Bull took full advantage. That hasn't been the case with Troy's Crispin Rice, who despite his four fouls hasn't backed off on defense.

Play-by-Play Man: McBride with the ball for the Spartans. Bacic right in front of him, all the way. It will be interesting to see how Red Bull negotiates those physical Michigan State screens, the type that put him out of action for several minutes. Here's one of those screens now. Grizzly Bear Cousins sets it high. McBride cuts around, shaking free of Bacic. A pair of Trojans converges on McBride. He shovels the ball to Cousins, who's fouled on the drive to the basket. Was that foul on Crispin Rice? If it is, he's finished for the night.

Color Commentator: There was a trio of Trojans surrounding Cousins on that drive—Boyce, Bacic, and Rice. And both Boyce and Bacic are raising their hands toward the scorer's table to say the foul was on them, trying to protect their teammate.

Play-by-Play Man: And after a short consultation, the referees point towards Aaron Boyce. They're saying the foul's on him. Coach Eddie Barker is furious on the Michigan State sideline. He's pointing towards Rice, slapping a hand down on his opposite wrist to say that's what he did, that's who fouled my player.

Color Commentator: If Barker had his voice and the refs could hear him, he might have picked up a technical right there. That foul is also Boyce's fourth of the game. One more and *he's* gone.

Play-by-Play Man: Here's the first foul shot by Grizzly Bear Cousins. It's short.

Color Commentator: These players are exhausted. There was very little from the legs on that free throw attempt. I'd venture to say that only McBride and the Red Bull have any explosiveness left.

Play-by-Play Man: The second shot. This one's too strong, long off the iron. The Trojans control the rebound.

Color Commentator: He overcompensated for the first shot being short. Just as Michigan State looked like they were going to pull away, they can't seal the deal.

Play-by-Play Man: Bacic with the ball. The crowd on their feet, a minute twelve to go. The Trojans trailing by two. And Red Bull eludes McBride. Michael Jordan has him now on the defensive switch. It's Bacic and Jordan. Jordan all over him. Bacic passes to Boyce. Boyce down low to Rice, who kicks it back out to Boyce. It's the smaller McBride on Boyce now. Boyce shoots over McBride and drains it from fifteen feet away. We're tied up at eighty-six. What a show! *What a show!*

Color Commentator: I'll tell you now—there's ice water in that young man's veins. He sent us into triple overtime with a bomb at the buzzer, and now he's tied this game up again.

Play-by-Play Man: There's fifty-six seconds on the game clock. Michigan State with the ball. If you're Eddie Barker, do you call time-out to regroup after losing a four-point lead?

Color Commentator: No, the momentum is clearly with Troy. Calling a time-out would let them feel it more. Plus the volatile freshman McBride is your go-to guy. You don't want him thinking on the sidelines or interacting with his teammates. You just want him to react on the court.

Play-by-Play Man: McBride over half-court with the ball. He jukes back and forth, trying to play matador with Red Bull. Now forty-six seconds on the game clock, twenty-five on the shot clock. A screen set by Baby Bear Wilkins—again the entire defense flows towards McBride. He kicks the ball off to Jordan. Jordan is open from twenty feet. He doesn't take the shot. Jordan back to McBride. Shot clock is down to twelve. McBride, in the face of two defenders, lets it fly. It's no good. They battle for the rebound. Crispin Rice pulls it away from Grizzly Bear Cousins. Troy has the ball. They can have the last shot if they want it. The shot clock is turned off with twenty-nine seconds to go. This could be an upset for the ages!

Color Commentator: Jordan should have pulled the trigger on that shot. Instead, he deferred to McBride. That's what happens when a team doesn't develop chemistry over the long haul.

Play-by-Play Man: Bacic on the dribble, letting the time run down.

Color Commentator: They want to start their assault on the

basket with about ten seconds to go. That gives them enough time to put in a loose rebound.

Play-by-Play Man: The ball goes to Rice, now back to Bacic. We're at eleven seconds now, the crowd at a fever pitch. Red Bull finds Boyce in the corner. He puts the ball on the floor, heading towards the basket. Michael Jordan takes away his lane. Boyce to Bacic. Three seconds. Rice is open beneath the rim, waving his arms. Now Bacic spots him. The pass. It's off Rice's fingertips *(buzzer sounds)* and time expires.

Color Commentator: That was the game if he catches that pass. Crispin Rice was left alone on the mad scramble. He's looking up at the basket now, staring at his hands. The Red Bull knew some-one was left open, because a sea of green was converging on him.

Play-by-Play Man: It didn't appear to be a *bad* pass. It was just an inch or so beyond Rice's reach.

Color Commentator: Rice could have ended this game and run into the arms of his fiancée on the biggest stage imaginable. But it wasn't meant to be. So we don't end triple overtime with a bang. But there are no whimpers here either. Just some tired legs on both sides and a big *whew* on the part of the Spartans, who sur-vived what could have been a game-ending miscommunication on defense.

"Don't give up. Don't ever give up."

—Jim Valvano, who coached North Carolina State University to perhaps the greatest upset in college basketball history, defeating heavily favored Houston at the buzzer in the 1983 NCAA Championship Game. He spoke these words less than two months before he died of cancer at the age of forty-seven.

CHAPTER TWENTY-THREE
CRISPIN RICE

8:01 P.M. (CT)

Crispin walks towards Roko, shaking his head.

"I blew it. I had it right on my fingers," says Crispin, gazing at his outstretched hand. "I anchored my feet to the floor and I couldn't move. So I had to reach for the ball."

"That was all on me, C-Rice. *I* screwed that up," replies Roko, standing directly in front of him and putting both hands on his shoulders. "I saw you there alone and I nearly jumped out of my skin trying to make that pass. I should have taken an extra breath, but I knew that time was running out."

"It was so close," says Crispin, hanging his head.

"Hey, we didn't lose anything yet," answers Roko with a burst of new energy. "We've got five more minutes to make this right, to show these Spartans who we really are. Now get your head up and let's go do this thing."

Troy's cheerleaders are performing out on the court now.

Crispin and Roko are forced to zigzag their way through them back to the Trojans' bench. Crispin's eyes are glued to the floor, trying to avoid eye contact with Hope. But the red-trimmed sneakers and bare ankles of the cheerleaders look nearly identical to him. And in his mind, Crispin has to make his way around a dozen Hopes, instead of facing her green eyes one-on-one.

MARCH, TWO AND A HALF WEEKS AGO

Crispin had arrived at practice nearly ninety minutes early. He was shooting alone at a side basket, trying to work the kinks out of his shot, when Coach Kennedy walked onto the court.

"Concentrate on keeping your right elbow tucked in. Every now and then, I see it flying out. I think it's really started to affect your consistency," said Kennedy as he moved towards him. "Your wrist and elbow always form a straight line. It doesn't matter what direction the rest of your body is falling. You can be leaning like the Tower of Pisa and still make shots. Everything hinges on the base beneath the ball being upright. It's the foundation that has to be strong."

"I'll watch out for it, Coach," said Crispin, with both hands resting on his knees, leaving him exactly at eye level with Kennedy.

"The other thing is that you look exhausted. You're sweating up a storm out here. This is supposed to be about touch, about feeling," said Kennedy, picking the rock up from the floor and letting it roll off his fingertips as a model. "I think you've become too tight, too mechanical. You're working against yourself. There's an old Chinese proverb: 'Don't try hard, try easy.' Maybe you've come across it making those food deliveries, inside of a fortune cookie or something."

"No, I don't read them," said Crispin through half a smile. "I just hand them out to customers who order from the Chinese side of the menu."

"Well, it's really true. You don't want to try *too* hard. Shooting a basketball is all about relaxation, focus, finding a rhythm."

"You think I've lost some of that?" asked Crispin.

"Absolutely. I could show you game film of when you were going good, before you got engaged. You were releasing the ball like there wasn't another thought on your mind," said Kennedy.

"I've probably been distracted lately," said Crispin, dobbing the sweat from his face with the bottom of his red and white reversible practice jersey.

"That's why I've been waiting to get you alone on the court, to talk about this," said Kennedy, walking closer to the rim. "Follow me. Get yourself five or six feet from the basket. I want you to get used to making shots again, not missing them. Work with just one ball, shot after shot. The rock shouldn't be in your hands for more than a second—keep it up in the air. Pick a song with some bounce to it. Play to the rhythm inside your head, like you were dancing out here."

So Crispin settled nearer to the hoop, and began humming to himself.

Then, with his hands and feet in constant motion, he started sinking short, easy shots, one after another.

"That's it. Let that good groove sink into your muscle memory, into your bones," said Kennedy, looking up at Crispin from beneath the basket. "I suppose it's pretty easy to get caught up in the whole media thing about America sharing in your marriage proposal, and the team's winning streak riding on this Hope of Troy nonsense. There's got to be a lot of pressure, trying to live up to that fairy-tale image."

"I've felt it," said Crispin in a more relaxed voice, as he continued shooting.

"We're all programmed not to fail, to be fearful of it. You and Hope put yourselves on a big stage, one that's very personal. Plenty of strangers' eyes watching, asking questions, giving advice. But you should trust your own eyes. Judge by what *you* see."

"You may not believe this, Coach," said Crispin, "but all of a sudden, I've got a lot to look at in that relationship."

Crispin thought back to the night before, when he and Hope finally spoke after their argument on the quad. They hadn't talked or texted each other in almost two days, the longest gap of time they'd gone without communicating since they started dating.

Crispin took the first step, showing up outside Hope's dorm just as she was getting back from a class.

"You want to figure this thing out with me, what's going on between us?" he asked in a calm voice.

"I do. I really do," she answered, coming up to within a foot or so of him.

"Well, what have you been thinking?"

"Honestly, I felt like you were accusing me of cheating to find a way out," Hope said. "That maybe you were too embarrassed to break up after proposing on TV."

"Really?" said Crispin, almost in disbelief.

"Tell me you haven't thought at least once about backing out."

After a moment of silence, Crispin conceded, "It's just because this is new territory to me. It has nothing to do with not being in love with you."

"Well, I've got some of those same feelings," said Hope, behind a deep breath.

Crispin nodded his head, and took a deep breath, too.

"Come on, let's go get some coffee or something," Hope said. "Let's try to get a better grip on all of this."

A few steps into the walk, Crispin reached for her hand.

The sound of the rock falling to the floor brought Crispin's mind back to the gym.

"The truth is, there's probably nothing to see in ourselves and our relationships that hasn't always been there," said Kennedy. "Sometimes we just get blinded by other things."

"I'll get back on point," said Crispin, picking the ball up. "I feel like I'm headed there already."

"One thing you haven't lost in this shooting slump, though,

is the respect of your teammates, especially Roko," emphasized Kennedy. "Every time you're open, he gets the ball into your hands."

"I won't let any of you down during the rest of the tournament," said Crispin.

Then, as Kennedy began walking away, he said, "The only way you could ever let us down is by quitting on yourself, thinking that you don't deserve better in life."

"I firmly believe that respect is a lot more important, and a lot greater, than popularity."

—Julius "Dr. J" Erving, NBA Champion and Hall of Famer

CHAPTER TWENTY-FOUR
MICHAEL JORDAN

8:01 P.M. (CT)

As MJ reaches the Spartans' bench, Coach Barker is waiting for him. He can see by the hard look on Barker's face that he has screwed up somehow.

He figures Barker is about to hang that blown defensive assignment on him and ream him out for leaving Crispin Rice alone beneath the basket.

Here it comes, that laryngitis voice about to torture my name again, MJ thinks to himself.

"Jordan, next time you get an open shot, take it!" strains Barker. "Don't be afraid to miss. Dealing with the hell of missing is part of the game."

"I hear you, Coach," says MJ.

"I don't give a damn what you *hear*," says Barker, poking a finger at MJ's head. "I only care what sinks into your brain."

Then MJ feels himself come under Malcolm's heavy glare. And if MJ had to put words to that look, it would be, *If you take a shot instead of me, you better make it.*

JANUARY, TWO MONTHS AGO

MJ couldn't get comfortable in his seat on the bus ride back to East Lansing, after the Spartans defeated interstate rival Michigan in Ann Arbor.

"Stop squirming around. I'm trying to chill," said Malcolm, kneeing the back of MJ's seat. "It's not like your body's sore. How long did you play tonight—two lousy minutes?"

"It's not about that, *star*. I go hard in the warm-ups, and then I get tight sitting on the bench," said MJ over his shoulder.

"You know how ridiculous that sounds?" sniped Malcolm, who always sat in the last seat on the bus, as far away from Barker's postgame speeches as he could get.

"Think he's squirming and uptight now?" said Grizzly Bear, with his legs stretched to the side over an empty seat. "You should have seen MJ two years ago, the night we played Illinois and they had Michael Jordan's son on their squad."

"That's right, I remember—Jeffrey Jordan, aka 'Heir Jordan,'" said Baby Bear, sitting behind Grizzly and opposite Malcolm. "MJ was all like, 'Which one is he?'"

"I warned MJ, 'If you ask the dude for his autograph, I'll kick your ass,'" recalled Grizzly.

"Jeffrey? That's MJ's middle name," said Malcolm with a smirk.

"I didn't know that shit," said Grizzly.

"Me neither," said Baby Bear.

And the three of them laughed hard over it as MJ scowled.

"Seeing him must have been like looking into a mirror for you," mocked Malcolm.

"Yeah, it was something like that," mumbled MJ, staring out the window.

"So, could Heir Jordan ball like his pops?" asked Malcolm.

"Nah, he wasn't even a starter," said Baby Bear. "He mostly rode the bench. I think he transferred from Illinois to some small school in Florida to play with his younger brother."

"Then what was all the fuss about?" Malcolm asked MJ. "He was no better than you. Playing two-on-two, me and you would have put a whupping on Jordan's kids."

"It was about him and me growing up under a microscope—with the same name and pressures on the court," said MJ, turning back to face the guys.

"Only Heir Jordan did it in a mansion with security guards, watching his father win NBA Championships and get down with the Looney Tunes in *Space Jam*," cracked Baby Bear.

"So did you actually get on the court against him, or was this all drama in your head?" asked Malcolm.

"I watched him during the warm-ups. He had his game

face screwed on super tight, so I didn't say anything to him," said MJ.

"Back in the day, his pops would have blown off any dude on the other team who wanted to yak before a game," said Grizzly. "That's the kind of hard-core competitor he was."

"I was thinking about that, too," said MJ. "Anyway, he played seven or eight minutes in the first half, but I didn't get in."

"What a surprise," said Malcolm.

"But in the second half, we were ahead by something like fifteen points with three minutes left. There was a stop in play and the other coach sent Jeffrey Jordan back on the court. Then Barker yelled at me, 'Go out there and guard him! Show him who his daddy is!'"

"Oh, Coach had jokes," said Malcolm, slapping his knee in amusement.

"And you have to remember, Heir Jordan doesn't have a single point in the game yet," adds Baby Bear for Malcolm's benefit.

"Almost right away, he gets the rock and I'm in front of him one-on-one," said MJ, with his shoulders starting to shift, as if he were playing now. "He fakes left and then right, but I don't budge. All of a sudden, he blasts straight at me. I had to take a step back on my heels, and he cut around. The only thing I could do was foul, but he scored anyway. Then he hit the foul shot for a three-point play."

"And our home crowd was into it, too. They knew it was Jordan-on-Jordan," said Grizzly Bear. "It was like a mini-game inside of our game."

"I would have tackled his ass before I let him score," Malcolm told MJ. "Did you get back at him?"

"I stopped him another time. Then I finally got the ball in my hands with, like, five seconds left, standing behind the three-point line. But we were ahead by ten points, and Coach told us to kill off the clock. So I just held onto the rock," said MJ. "After the game, I wanted to fist-bump him. But he was already heading back down the tunnel towards the lockers."

"I'll tell you this right now," said Malcolm. "Me and you come from two different planets. Because sure as anything, I would have shot that three-pointer to get even."

"See, that's the difference between us," said MJ. "It's not all about me—my wants, my wishes. It's about the team."

"I heard that crap a million times—there's no *I* in team," said Malcolm. "It don't matter how much I play it for myself; you're still my brother on the court. I've got your back over any dude wearing a different color. I would have knocked Jordan Jr. on his royal ass to get you an open shot. Coach should have had your back the same way."

"Wait, let me get this straight. You're my *brother* on the court? You're my *brother* on this team?" asked MJ, with his voice slowing down twice to punctuate the same word. "Since when?"

"It's not my fault you don't see it. Maybe none of you do," said Malcolm, expanding his gaze from MJ to Grizzly and Baby Bear, too. "See, you want me to be your *little* brother. My skills make me *big* brother to all of you. So when they put the plate of pork chops out on the table, I grab first. Take as much as I want. You all come after. That's respect for me. The respect I deserve here."

Grizzly and Baby Bear laughed, shaking their heads at each other, like Malcolm was full of bull.

But MJ looked at Malcolm and thought to himself, "At least that's something I can wrap my mind around. I don't completely agree with it—maybe not even fifty percent worth. But I understand where he's coming from a little more now."

"[T]he NCAA criminalizes normal behavior."

—Jay Bilas, a lawyer, TV analyst, and former college basketball player

CHAPTER TWENTY-FIVE
MALCOLM McBRIDE

8:03 P.M. (CT)

As Troy's opening shot of the fourth overtime glances off the rim, Malcolm takes off, fast-breaking alone up the court. He knows it's a gamble. That without him boxing out Red Bull, the Trojans have an extra man to try and grab an offensive rebound and score. But by releasing early, Malcolm easily sneaks behind the Trojan defense.

MJ outhustles a pair of Trojans, rebounding the ball for Michigan State. In an instant, he catches sight of Malcolm running ahead of the field.

Then MJ delivers a bullet pass, hitting Malcolm between the numbers in full stride.

Even while dribbling the rock, Malcolm is flat out the fastest player on the court. He's already several steps ahead of his nearest defender and pulling farther away.

Nearing the foul line, Malcolm is preparing to explode out of his shoes.

He wants to tear down the iron with a slam dunk that will shake the Superdome, and the Trojans' confidence.

Planting his left foot, Malcolm cups the rock inside his right hand, securing it with his powerful wrist and forearm.

With the camera shutters clicking and the roar of the fans building in his ears, Malcolm leaps forward. And just as he's ready to pound the rock home, he reaches back for something more, to punish the rim for every trial his family has ever been put through.

But that glint of revenge throws Malcolm off by a mere millimeter.

His dunk rings off the back of the iron, and the rock ricochets twenty feet into the air as if it had wings.

Malcolm's momentum carries him past the basket and out of bounds.

And the ball lands in the hands of Roko Bacic, who leads his Trojan teammates in the opposite direction.

MARCH, NEARLY FOUR WEEKS AGO

As Malcolm walked off the court after basketball practice, he noticed Coach Barker eyeing him. He was beat tired and wasn't in the mood to hear Barker bitch about the inbounds play he'd screwed up. So Malcolm bowed his head and tried to walk past.

"McBride," said Barker, who called Malcolm by his last name whenever he was pissed at him. "I received a text from Ms. Thad. She'd like to see you in her office in fifteen minutes."

"Coach, I'm too spent to fill out any kind of paperwork now," said Malcolm, running a fresh towel across his forehead.

"Paperwork, huh? I hope that's *all* it is," said Barker, pounding a ball against the floor. "Get it taken care of, pronto. I don't care if you have to crawl there."

Malcolm watched the slits of Barker's eyes grow sharper and asked, "There something more I should know about this?"

"Just go see Ms. Thad, McBride," grumbled Barker. "I'll let her do her job before I have anything to add."

Then, without saying another word, Barker walked over to the free-throw line, where he started shooting foul shots by himself.

After Malcolm showered and left the locker room, he crossed the street to the athletic administration building and climbed a flight of marble stairs.

A secretary sitting in an outer office told Malcolm that Ms. Thad was waiting for him.

The letters on the frosted glass read

MS. THAD
DIRECTOR OF COMPLIANCE

Malcolm knocked on the wooden doorframe surrounding it.

"Enter," came a voice from inside, and Malcolm cracked the

door open just wide enough to stick his head through.

"You wanted to see me for something?"

"Yes, Malcolm. Thanks for getting here so quickly," said Ms. Thad in an easygoing voice. "Step inside, please."

In the six months Malcolm had been at Michigan State, Ms. Thad had talked to him a couple of times about his scholarship paperwork, and she'd given the whole team a speech once about all the little NCAA rules you could break by accident.

She was an absolute hottie, probably in her early thirties. She usually wore skirts that hung just above her knees. So when she spoke, everybody on the team listened—and watched.

Ms. Thad stood up to shake Malcolm's hand. When she sat back down behind her desk, and her legs disappeared from his view, Malcolm's focus shifted to the framed photo of a brown and white pit bull on the windowsill behind her.

"Have a seat, Malcolm. I'm afraid that I have some difficult questions for you. I take it you understand the meaning of illegal benefits for student athletes?"

"*Illegal?* You mean against the real law, or against the NCAA law?" asked Malcolm, settling himself into a soft leather chair.

"The NCAA doesn't have put-you-in-jail kinds of laws. It has bylaws—rules and regulations that we have to follow," she said, pointing to a thick NCAA manual sitting on the corner of her desk. "I received a phone call today from a reporter who's quite friendly towards MSU. This reporter gave me a heads-up that his newspaper is in the process of gathering information about a possible story concerning your family receiving illegal benefits because of your position here on the basketball team."

"That's crazy. I don't have a car, money, a job, or nothing like that. My parents drive the same old wreck, live in the exact same apartment. My father may even be getting laid off soon."

"That's what makes this so unusual and sensitive," said Ms. Thad, who picked up a pen and a long yellow legal pad to take notes. "This doesn't have to do with taking money, cars, a job, or a house. Unfortunately, I need to ask you about your sister's headstone in Elmwood Cemetery."

"What?" responded Malcolm, sitting up straighter. "What did you just say to me?"

"I know it's difficult, but here's my question to you. Was the headstone paid for by your parents?"

Malcolm slumped back in his chair and thought for a minute. Then, in a quiet voice, he said, "That's their daughter. They paid for everything. The funeral. The grave plot. A headstone. My parents had to spread that kind of money out over three different credit cards."

"I'm sure they did. But is that the *same* headstone standing there now?"

After a long pause, Malcolm hung his head and answered, "No, it's not. But why don't you just leave this all alone?"

"Malcolm, it's my job to get to the truth. I represent this university. My position is to protect MSU, to find violations that could potentially embarrass us. I'm sorry, but I have to ask you a few more questions concerning this matter."

Suddenly, Malcolm felt like there was a pit bull behind that desk in front of him—a pit bull in stockings—to go with the photo on the windowsill.

"When was a headstone first erected?"

"I guess that would be in September of my senior year in high school, almost a year and a half ago," answered Malcolm. "I remember because I had the tattoo of Trisha on my arm already, and I got that in August."

"The original headstone? The one your parents paid for?"

"Yes," said Malcolm, followed by a long breath.

"And when was the new one erected?"

"I'm not sure. The first time I saw it was that November, just about two months later. It was right after Thanksgiving."

Ms. Thad flipped through the calendar on her desk.

"So that's more than a year ago—approximately sixteen months. And you'd already committed to play at MSU by then?"

"That's right."

"Were your parents surprised the first time they saw the new headstone there?"

"Yeah, my father was. I was there with him. He didn't know about it. But there are lots of people who loved my sister. It could have been a gift from the marching band at our high school, or somebody rich who wanted to stay anonymous and do a good deed."

"What about your mother, Malcolm? Was she surprised by it?"

"I guess. My father was the one who told her. After that, she wouldn't talk about it. None of us would."

"I see."

"My parents didn't go around trying to find out who did it. They just accepted it."

"That probably would have been fine," said Ms. Thad, with her pen flying across the pad. "Only it turns out that the newspaper found a receipt for that headstone paid for by Detroit's biggest sports agent, someone who represents several current NBA players. And that agent's brother happens to be in a church choir with your mother."

"I've never been contacted by anybody like that. And neither have my parents. They would have told me for sure."

"Look, right now there's no newspaper article. Things like that usually take a lot of time. They like to have multiple sources and check every fact to the umpteenth degree before they print. And there's no NCAA investigation yet either. A headstone isn't normally perceived as a gift. So maybe nothing's going to come of this at all. But MSU needs to be prepared. I may have more questions for you at a later time. But for now, don't speak to anyone about this."

"Does Coach know?"

"He knows as much as I just told you."

"What's the worst thing that could happen to me over something like this?" asked Malcolm. "I'd lose my eligibility? I couldn't play in the NCAA Tournament next week?"

"No, penalties would never come that fast. An investigation would most likely take several months, maybe a year," said Ms. Thad. "I imagine you'd be in the NBA by then. MSU, the basketball program, and Coach Barker would eventually pay the price. You'd be free and clear of the NCAA's authority."

"And that's supposed to make me feel good? Because it doesn't!" said Malcolm, getting up from his chair and then walking towards the frosted glass door. "I don't need these headaches. None of us do. And over what? Nothing!"

> *"[Basketball is] now a game for the whole world."*
>
> —Vlade Divac, a humanitarian and one of the first
> Eastern European players to compete in the NBA

CHAPTER TWENTY-SIX
ROKO BACIC

8:05 P.M. (CT)

With 3:10 remaining and the game still knotted up, Roko gets stripped of the ball by Malcolm's lightning-swift hands. He tries to banish the thought of that turnover from his mind. It gets easier to do with the Spartans flying down the court in a wave, intent on seizing the lead. You can't be a good point guard or a good defender without having a short memory, without the ability to forget about your last mistake.

In the span of just a few backpedaling strides, Roko's thoughts become clear and focused as he searches for an angle to cut off Malcolm's dribble.

To Roko's left, Aaron arrives to double-team Malcolm,

convinced he has no intention of passing the ball. That causes Roko to instantly readjust his calculations, and slightly turn his body.

Roko and Aaron hang like a crimson shadow over Malcolm as he attacks the hoop on a driving layup.

When Malcolm extends the rock in his right hand, both defenders go for the block. And for an instant, the hands of all three players are touching the ball.

The ref's whistle blows for a foul on the Trojans.

"That was perfect defense!" screams Coach Kennedy from the sideline. "We tied him up! Where was the contact? You let *them* play like thugs, and we can't breathe on anybody!"

Roko raises his hand to say it's on him. But the ref shakes his head, pointing at Aaron. It's his fifth and final foul, so Aaron is now out of the game.

"That's it," says Malcolm. "We're going to pull their team apart piece by piece."

The Superdome crowd gives Aaron a standing ovation as he walks off the court. But the loudest applause is coming from his family and friends behind the Trojans' bench. And Roko, along with his red-wigged surrogate parents, claps his hands harder and harder for him.

A moment later, Malcolm sets his feet at the free-throw line.

Putting that blown breakaway dunk behind him, he buries both foul shots.

The Spartans lead the Trojans 88–86.

March 29 (two days ago)
This morning I walked into the Superdome for
the first time. I couldn't believe its incredible size.
Maybe it's big enough to land a jumbo jet inside,
or build a small city beneath its roof. Before
we went to our locker room to change, Coach
Kennedy arranged for Aaron, his mother, and his
aunt and uncle to take us on a special tour. They
brought us to section III and we all sat down in
the seats there. That's the section where Aaron
and his family stayed for two days and nights to
survive Hurricane Katrina, back in the summer of
2005, when Aaron was fourteen years old. I knew
it was going to be a serious talk from the heart
because it was the only time that Aaron's aunt and
uncle (my official parents in New Orleans) took off
their red curly wigs. So I pulled out a pen and my
notebook.

Aaron wanted his mother to speak. But she
said, "These are your teammates. You share a
bond with them that I don't. They need to hear
about what happened from you." So Aaron told us
about his first morning here. How it started out
almost as a great adventure. "I kept looking at
the football field on the floor, where the basketball
court is laid out now. I couldn't believe I was
sitting here for free. It was like a dream," said

Aaron. Then he told about how fast that dream turned into a living nightmare, like the Freddy Krueger character from the movies was suddenly turned loose on the thousands of people seeking shelter inside the Superdome.

"First thing—boom, the AC stopped working. It got to be like 120 degrees in here with all the heat and humidity. Then more and more people came, lots of them in bad shape from the storm, adding more body heat. There were crazy long lines to get food. National Guard soldiers with machine guns handed out box lunches. Then they ran out of supplies and people started fighting over whatever food and water they could get their hands on," Aaron said.

Aaron's uncle told him not to forget about the bathrooms. But his uncle got so upset just mentioning it that he started to tell that part himself. "All the toilets backed up when the water pressure dropped, because of the floods in the streets. That stink was everywhere in the Superdome. You couldn't escape it. You couldn't step into a bathroom without getting sick to your stomach. So people started relieving themselves in every corner of this place," said his uncle, sounding as angry as if it had happened yesterday.

When he said that, I thought about those

terrible times as a small boy in Zagreb. The nights
we hid in my neighbor's basement overnight with
no bathroom, because of the exploding mortar
shells outside.

Finally, Aaron's mother spoke. She said, "It
wasn't all evil. There were some beautiful things
that happened here too. They were things that
would really touch your heart, like people doing
good deeds for complete strangers, treating them
like family, and sharing the last of their food and
drink with the sickly and senior citizens. But lots
of elderly folks died in the heat waiting for medical
help. And none of us trapped here knew for sure
if we'd have a home to go back to, or if our city
would be completely washed away, killing off our
culture, our roots. One of the only things that
eased my mind was the fact that the football team
that plays in this stadium is named the Saints. I
took that as a sign and a blessing."

Coach Kennedy stood up from his seat, like he
was a student and Aaron's mother was a professor.
He asked her, "How do you feel when you look
around the Superdome now and see all of it put
back together, knowing your son will play here in
the Final Four?" She thought about it for a few
seconds and then said, "Part of me feels a real
sense of triumph for my family and the people

of New Orleans. Another part of me looks at the
free tickets we got for the game and says that
isn't nearly enough to make up for what we went
through in this Superdome. So it's all very mixed
emotions for me. I guess I'm optimistic, grateful,
and bitter all at the same time."

As we left, I looked around at that perfect
stadium and the hundreds of workers polishing
things up like new for the Final Four. I thought
about Croatia and wondered if my country would
ever get put back together.

Maybe the souls of New Orleans and Zagreb
are not so different.

Maybe Aaron is closer to being my brother
than I ever knew.

"If you make every game a life-and-death proposition, you're going to have problems. For one thing, you'll be dead a lot."

—Dean Smith, who coached the University of North Carolina for thirty-six years, winning two NCAA Championships and reaching the Final Four eleven times

CHAPTER TWENTY-SEVEN
CRISPIN RICE

8:07 P.M. (CT)

Without the threat of the sharpshooting Aaron in the lineup, the Spartans blanket Crispin and Roko, stifling the Trojans' offense. As the shot clock winds down, Crispin is forced into a tough off-balance floater in the lane. Michigan State hauls in the rebound. They head up court with Malcolm in control of the ball, looking to increase their two-point lead with 2:35 remaining.

Crispin is battling Grizzly Bear Cousins for position down low.

Then, suddenly, Grizzly steps out to set a hard screen on Roko.

The pair collides and the referee whistles Roko for the foul, his fourth of the game.

Coach Kennedy leaps off the bench and onto the court to argue the call.

"There's no way that's on us!" screams Kennedy, whose right arm slips loose from his suit jacket's sleeve. "That's bullshit! Fouls? All game long they've been getting away with felonies!"

Crispin sees his coach yank his other arm from its sleeve and fling his jacket to the floor.

That's when Crispin jumps in front of Kennedy, pulling him away from the referee.

The ref has the whistle in his mouth and his hands ready to make the letter T.

The only things saving Kennedy from a technical foul and free throws by the Spartans is the ref's patience and Crispin's grip on his coach.

As Kennedy starts to simmer down and Crispin relaxes his hold, the coach tells him, "Don't waste your strength. You're going to need every bit of it on the court."

"It's no sweat, Coach," says Crispin. "You'd do the same for me."

YESTERDAY

Sitting in the middle of a semicircle, surrounded by his team-mates in their locker room, Crispin carefully taped his hurting right pinkie to his ring finger for support.

Hearing Coach Kennedy clear his throat, Crispin focused his eyes on the center of the room.

"Coach Barker has more experience than I do. He's been here before and won. So somewhere along the line I'll probably cost us a point or two. And the rest of you will have to make up for that," said Coach Kennedy, taking a step closer to his players and leaving the Xs and Os on the board behind him. "The Spartans' biggest advantage is Malcolm McBride. He's the best athlete on the court. But their biggest disadvantage can also be McBride. Sometimes he doesn't get it. He thinks the basketball belongs to him, that it has *his* name on it."

Crispin held the tape taut with his teeth, and then he ripped it from the roll, before pulling the piece even tighter around that pair of fingers.

"So Mr. One and Done never heard that Phil Jackson quote you're always pushing?" asked Aaron. "The one that goes, 'Basketball is sharing.'"

"If he has heard it, apparently it's never made much of an impression on him," said Kennedy.

"Coach, you think we can *help* him to feel that way—that the rock is really his?" asked Roko, from Crispin's immediate left.

"I'll bet Roko can do it. And maybe the *Red Bull* can bring it out in McBride even more," said Crispin, to the murmuring approval of his teammates.

"You guys might be on to something," said Kennedy, with a grin. "But don't become overly concerned with McBride, or the size of their big men. Remember, our biggest plus is *us*. We've been looking after each other since the beginning of the season, way before we ever got this far. We believed in each other before anybody outside of this room ever did. That means we were winners before our record proved it. Just don't get caught up in the media hype that this moment is too big for a team from Troy, Alabama."

That's when a player shouted out one of the clichés he'd read about his team's chances. "They're content just to be here."

Then a few more voices followed after him.

"This experience is something Troy can build on next year."

"Cinderella's always gone before midnight."

"Will they melt in the glare of the national stoplight?"

"I see you guys have been reading your own press. That can be a dangerous thing," said Kennedy. "The reporters who write those stories—they're outsiders. They don't really know us or how we'll respond to the pressure. Crispin, you're a senior. You've seen this team take shape over the past four years. How do you think we'll respond?"

"I think that any pressure will disappear once the game starts. We'll just clear our minds and we'll be in the flow."

"I agree. By the way, Crispin tells me he has an announcement to share with the team," said Kennedy.

Crispin took a deep breath, looking around him, from side to side, before he spoke again.

"There's been a lot of attention on this 'Hope of Troy' thing. How Hope's been our good luck charm and stuff. I wanted to say something here that's private, intended for our ears only," said Crispin, squeezing the five fingers on his right hand together. "This morning, Hope and I decided to put our engagement off for a while. Neither one of us is really ready for it. I wanted you to hear it from me. And to know that it's not going to affect my play. We're a team, and a good one, too. That's how we got this far. We don't need good luck charms. We just need to continue to play together, and support each other on the court."

"You'll have our support, always," said Roko, touching a closed fist to Crispin's left biceps. "We're more than a team here. We're a family."

Then other voices echoed that feeling through the locker room.

"Win or lose, brothers to the end."

"Yeah, we're here for you, Crisp. All of us."

*"If all I'm remembered for is being a good basketball player,
then I've done a bad job with the rest of my life."*

—Isiah Thomas, former NCAA and NBA Champion

CHAPTER TWENTY-EIGHT
MICHAEL JORDAN

8:09 P.M. (CT)

MJ shadows his man on defense as the Spartans protect a
slim two-point lead. Then, out of the corner of his eye, he
sees Red Bull slip free from Malcolm, beginning his drive
to the basket. Without hesitation, MJ slides over into Roko's path,
leaving his man alone. But as MJ commits himself, he sees Roko's
eyes shift to the open spot on the court that MJ just left.

Roko delivers the ball to MJ's wide-open man.

No Spartan helps out to cover him, and MJ can only sprint
back there, too late to stop the shot.

"Stay with *your* man, not mine!" Malcolm roars at MJ as the
ball rips through the netting. "Know your place out here! Find it
and stay there!"

With the score now tied 88–88 with 1:45 left, the Spartans advance the ball.

The Trojans are focused on Malcolm, waiting for him to jet to the basket.

Coach Barker holds two palms out in front of him, telling his team to take their time. Malcolm passes off to his teammates, with the rock always coming right back into his hands.

As the shot clock ticks down to ten seconds, Malcolm gets more serious about his coming assault on the rim. His final pass is to MJ, whose defender has backed way off of him, cheating towards Malcolm.

Then, with the memory of Barker's speech about taking the open shot scorched into his brain, MJ fakes the pass back to Malcolm.

The feint buys him even more room, and MJ takes a long breath before he goes into his shooting motion.

MJ blocks out everything around him—Malcolm, the defenders, the crowd, and even how much that one shot means.

Gliding off his fingertips, the ball feels almost weightless to MJ.

The crowd noise explodes in his ears as the Spartans regain the lead.

LAST NIGHT

MJ was looking out a window at the lights of New Orleans when Malcolm stepped out of his bedroom in the hotel suite they were sharing.

"My own bedroom and my own toilet—now this is class," said

Malcolm, wearing a green sweat suit and walking barefoot. "Not like that joke of a room they give us in the athletes' dorm—four walls, two beds, two desks, one cramped toilet."

"Better get used to luxury. You're going to be a multimillionaire in about three months," said MJ, who addressed Malcolm's reflection in the window without turning around. "But you're not the only lucky one. I'll be improving my living conditions, too, you know."

"Yeah, how's that?"

"I'm getting a room of my own in the dorms, doubling my space. I figure you're moving out after the championship game on Monday night," said MJ. "You'll sign with a big sports agency, and they'll rent you out a mansion and a sports car until the draft comes and you've got dough of your own to throw around."

"I'll move my parents into that mansion before you can blink," said Malcolm, going over to the window himself and looking out beside MJ. "That's a lot of lights from clubs and hotels. Do they have any project buildings here in New Orleans?"

"They've got plenty of poor people, so I'm sure they do—projects and homeless shelters," said MJ. "Hey, I was impressed by what you said today to those reporters. I actually agree with you for once. The college basketball system *is* a rip-off for the players."

"I don't have time to think about that now," said Malcolm. "It's all about taking down Troy."

"So from your comments I guess you won't be donating a bunch of money to the MSU athletic department, as a thank-you for getting you into the pros," said MJ.

"That's right. Michigan State didn't do a damn thing for me," said Malcolm, with his voice gathering momentum. "I put money in the school's pocket, in Coach's pocket, the sneaker company's. They ought to build a statue of me, instead of me ever giving them money."

"Well, what are you going to do with all that money? Something for kids who live in the projects?" asked MJ.

"You know what? I'd really like to. But I don't do favors for people," said Malcolm. "Doing a favor's what robbed us of my sister. That's a line I can't cross."

"Yeah, but it's like you said to me one time—it's not a favor if they don't ask. So you offer."

Malcolm opened his mouth to argue, then he closed it again. He just looked out the window silently for a while.

"Well, I guess I could see kids all over Brewster-Douglass wearing my pro jersey if I built something like a rec center. Then they wouldn't have to play ball on the street all the time, dodging the drama that jumps up out of nowhere. But still, I don't like the idea of giving money away."

"*Freshman*, think about it. The government is going to take at least thirty percent of what you make in taxes. Only they haven't got a clue how to spend that money right. And I'll prove it to you. Ever see anything change in your neighborhood? See things get any better?"

"Not where I'm from, and especially not for kids," answered Malcolm. "Even when my sister went to China with her high school band, that money came from people all over the projects in ones, fives, and ten-dollar bills."

"So you and your lawyers create a foundation. Most of that same money the government was going to take, you can spend it any way you want, like on that rec center you just thought about. You and your parents can do something in your sister's name."

"You know, I kind of like that idea. The Trisha McBride Foundation for Youth," said Malcolm, tapping at his own image in the glass.

"Think about it."

"I will," said Malcolm, before he paused. "Not that I ever wanted a college roommate. But if I had to have one, you've been all right. You even made an impression on me here and there."

"And I think I can say my respect for you has grown," said MJ. "Anyway, the man your father named you after, Malcolm X—he probably would have been proud of what you said at that news conference today."

"Why's that?" asked Malcolm. "I know X didn't play college ball."

"Because you challenged the system, you *stand* for something now," said MJ. "You know what X said?"

"No, what?"

"He said, 'If you don't stand for something, you'll fall for anything.'"

LIVE RADIO BROADCAST OF THE GAME
8:10 P.M. (CT)

There are three broadcasters: a play-by-play man, a color commentator, and sideline reporter Rachel Adams.

Play-by-Play Man: A *new* Michael Jordan making his own mark on this game with that shot! It's Michigan State by a basket, ninety to eighty-eight. The clock down to a minute ten. Bacic with the ball for the Trojans.

Color Commentator: That's seventy seconds, the same number on the Trojans' sneakers. Is that some kind of fate?

Play-by-Play Man: Bacic passes to Rice down low. Rice passes out to the corner. Inside of one minute to play. The Trojans now get it back to Roko Bacic. McBride in front of him. Bacic on the drive. The running one-hander. It's good! He banked it in off the glass with McBride all over him! We're tied at ninety!

Color Commentator: Tremendous defense by McBride. I can't fault it. Just a better shot by the Bull, taking the only option he was given.

Play-by-Play Man: The crowd is frenetic. Could we see a fifth overtime? McBride is on the dribble. Bacic confronts him, contesting McBride for every inch of court now.

Color Commentator: I have a feeling these two will—

Play-by-Play Man: And Bacic steals the ball! He just took it from McBride! He has a half-step on him for the hoop. He lays it in and scores. Bacic scores off the steal. The Trojans are in front ninety-two to ninety. Just thirty-four seconds remain. The shot clock is turned off.

Color Commentator: McBride blew that breakaway dunk early in this fourth overtime, and now that steal. He's going to have a lot to live with if the Spartans can't rally from here.

Play-by-Play Man: McBride with the ball. Bacic is hounding him. He got a hand on the ball and almost stole it again. Bacic nearly swiped the ball again, but McBride recovers. Now Baby Bear Wilkins screens for McBride. Bacic can't fight through. Crispin Rice runs at McBride now. Sixteen seconds to play. A mismatch, with Rice guarding the smaller, quicker McBride. And now Michael Jordan bumps Rice. McBride's free. He steps back for a long three. Bull's-eye! The Spartans lead by one, ninety-three to ninety-two! There are eleven seconds left to play, and the Trojans call time-out.

Color Commentator: That's guts. McBride's still standing on the court talking to his right hand, with the game clock frozen on his uniform number—eleven. But instead of having a conversation with his hand, McBride should be thanking the rear end of

Michael Jordan for bumping Rice. That's what ultimately got McBride free.

Play-by-Play Man: If you're coach Alvin Kennedy, if you're coach Eddie Barker, what do you do now?

Color Commentator: I think you pray. You thank your lucky stars for being a part of this game. But beyond that, you want to keep your team alert. Anything can happen out there. It already has and it probably will again. You tell them—no spectators, no one standing around, everyone involved until the final whistle blows.

Play-by-Play Man: Both teams seemed exhausted at the end of forty minutes of regulation time. But now this game is more than three hours old. They've played just eleven seconds shy of four additional five-minute overtimes. That's nearly sixty minutes of game clock, not to mention the emotional exhaustion as well.

Color Commentator: At this point there's no such thing as exhaustion for these players. There's just the will to win. One team is going on to the National Championship Game in forty-eight hours; the other team is going home. That's enough to carry them forward. I just feel sorry that the poet Homer didn't get a chance to chronicle *this* Trojan War.

Play-by-Play Man: The Spartans and Trojans are exiting their respective huddles, and the crowd gives them both a tremendous round of applause. Come to think of it, the fans of these two schools must be as drained as the players. And I'm told we have an update from Rachel Adams on the sidelines.

Rachel Adams: Yes, I had a chance to listen in a bit on both huddles. It was calm and relaxed on the Trojans bench with coach Alvin Kennedy diagramming several options for plays. But on the other bench, coach Eddie Barker was pushing the last of his voice to the limits. And he said something I've never heard a coach say before: "Their team doesn't know how to win a game this big. They only know how to lose." In just trying to interpret the feeling on each bench, if I didn't know the score, I'd think the Trojans were ahead by a point and not the Spartans.

Play-by-Play Man: Interesting stuff, Rachel.

Color Commentator: We'll see if that Trojan calmness, inspired by Alvin Kennedy, translates into something big for his squad.

Play-by-Play Man: The referee's ready to begin play. The crowd is up on their feet. The reserves from both benches are standing as well. In the tunnel, the players from Duke and North Carolina are straining to see who survives this epic war.

Color Commentator: Some of the players on this court have lived their whole lives to bring something special to these eleven seconds.

Play-by-Play Man: Here we go. Crispin Rice to inbound. He gets the ball to Roko Bacic. Bacic drives left. McBride's glued to him. We're down to eight seconds. Bacic with a small seam. He attacks the rim and arches a shot high over McBride's reach. It doesn't go. Three seconds. The rebound is batted around, tapped loose by Jordan. One second. Tapped by Rice—no. A second tap at it by Rice *(buzzer sounding)*. It's in! Rice tipped it in! Oh my! But did he beat the buzzer? One referee's saying yes it counts. Another referee is waving it off, saying no, it doesn't count. The players don't know what to do—celebrate or mourn. Everything's on hold. It's suddenly turned stone silent here in the Superdome, with everyone waiting for the replay and for the officials to confer.

Color Commentator: Rice hasn't run over to Hope Daniels, like he did when he made that game-winning basket at the buzzer earlier this season. He's probably not sure if he got it off in time either. In fact, there's only one thing for sure: there won't be another overtime. Either the Spartans or the Trojans have won this game by a single point.

Play-by-Play Man: Here's the replay on the scoreboard. Rice tips it just as the game clock reads zeros across the board. Boy, that's close. The officials are now huddled at a television monitor at the scorer's table, watching it in slow motion.

Color Commentator: And right behind those officials are Crispin Rice, Roko Bacic, Michael Jordan, and Malcolm McBride. Those players have seen the scoreboard replay. They're not sure either. And now they're looking at each other, the four of them. There's nothing between them except a few feet of space. No more pretenses. No more posturing. It doesn't get any purer than this. They don't know who won or who lost. They just know they've been through some incredible journey *together*.

Play-by-Play Man: I was just a spectator to it all and I feel it. I can only imagine what it's like for them.

Color Commentator: They've been a part of something much bigger than themselves. Something you can't put a label on. If I could freeze this moment in time for them, I would. I'd let them walk away with what they share right now, before it gets fractured by an outcome. But that's not how we play this game. There's always a winner, and there's always a loser.

Friday, April 5: From a national newspaper:

PHENOM FACES PAST
AND A FRESH START

NEW ORLEANS, La.—For 18-year-old basketball phenom Malcolm McBride, the past week has been a roller-coaster ride of tremendous highs and lows.

Last Saturday night, McBride, a freshman at Michigan State, led the Spartans to a dramatic

93–92 quadruple-overtime win over the Trojans of Troy at the Final Four in the Louisiana Super-dome. But the celebration didn't last long. The next morning, an article appeared in a Michigan news-paper detailing how a Detroit-based sports agent named Rodney Crowell had footed the bill for a lavish headstone at the grave site of McBride's sis-ter, Trisha, who was killed in a drive-by shooting nearly three years ago.

That gift may eventually cause McBride to be deemed ineligible under NCAA rules for receiving improper benefits, and possibly result in Michigan State forfeiting part or all of their wins this sea-son, as well as suffering future penalties.

Then, on Monday, the day of the National Championship Game between North Carolina and Michigan State, the NCAA announced it would formally investigate the connection between the McBride family and Crowell, whose brother is a member of the same church choir as Malcolm's mother, Florence McBride.

"My mother would never do anything wrong like that. Never. If anything, she was a target, and got fooled," said Malcolm McBride, who has already left Michigan State and relocated with his family to Florida to train for the upcoming NBA combine (where coaches and scouts evaluate top college prospects) and enter the league's draft this June.

"I've never even met this Rodney Crowell dude," said McBride, as he stood inside a Miami gym, dressed in shorts and a tank top, with a basketball tucked beneath one arm. "And I've just signed with a different agent, so there never was a connection, or a bribe gift by him. But that whole story was a distraction for my team."

Whether it was because of the distraction of the impending NCAA investigation or the four overtimes against the resilient Trojans, the Spartans showed up at the National Championship Game without their legs. They were blown out by the North Carolina Tar Heels from start to finish in a 91–64 defeat, a game in which an exhausted-looking McBride scored only 14 points, his lowest output of the tournament.

"I tried my best for Michigan State and my teammates. I care about Coach [Eddie Barker] and all of those guys. I'm sorry if they'll have to deal with any of this in the future. It's not right," said an emotional McBride. "In the end, my time there meant more to me than I thought it would. I guess that's what happens when players suffer together. And that's what our last two games together were—suffering to win, and suffering to lose."

Then McBride pulled a bandage from his left biceps, revealing a brand-new tattoo, one opposite the portrait of his sister's face, which occupies his right biceps. The tattoo reads SPARTANS FOREVER IN THE TROJAN WAR, with the letters encircling a flaming basketball.

"Success is never final, failure is never fatal. It's courage that counts."

—John Wooden, a Hall of Fame basketball player and coach who
guided UCLA to ten NCAA Championships over a twelve-year span

Looking for more courtside action?
Keep reading for a sample of
Paul Volponi's award-winning novel

BLACK

I admit it. I've been scared shitless lots of times. But I was never as shook as when the gun in Eddie's hand went off. It thundered inside that car like the whole world was coming to an end. I never expected Eddie to pull the trigger, by accident or any other way. I guess that was a big part of it, too. In all the time Eddie had that gun, we never shot it off once. It was just for show, so we could get our hands on some quick money. That's all. We never flashed it around in front of our friends or anything. It was just for us to know about.

I was more scared for that man we shot than anything else. I didn't even know he got clipped in the head until Eddie told me later. The gun went off and I closed my eyes. I shut them so tight, I thought my eyelids would squeeze them right out of their sockets. I only opened them again to find the handle on the door, so I could get out of that car and take off running.

That damn sound was ringing in my ears. There was no way to outrun that. I couldn't hear the air pumping in and out of my lungs, or the sound of my feet hitting against the concrete. And I didn't know that Eddie wasn't right behind me until I was halfway home, and peeked back over my shoulder. Then I looked back for him again, even though I knew he wasn't there.

I ran to my crib on instinct, and I guessed Eddie did the same. But I wished he was right there with me to explain what happened. I had to know right then. My brain was going twice as fast as my feet. I didn't know how to slow it down or what to think about first. I just needed to tell Eddie I had seen that man someplace before. I could still see his round, black face in front of me, like he was somebody I passed on the streets a hundred times. And I was praying to God with every breath I took that the man wasn't dead.

My name is Marcus Brown, but almost everybody outside my family calls me "Black." That's because they're used to seeing me all the time with my boy, Eddie Russo. Eddie is white. Kids who are different colors don't get to be that tight in my neighborhood. But we got past all that racial crap, until we were almost like real blood brothers. So somebody came up with the tag "Black and White" for us, and it stuck. It got more hype because we played basketball and football for Long Island City High School. We were two of the best players they ever had. Everybody who goes there knows about us. We even made the newspapers for winning big games a couple of times. Scouts from lots of colleges came to see us play. Some of them wanted to sign up the both of us, and keep what we had going. But that's all finished with now.

I don't remember if the idea of robbing people came up before Eddie snuck out his dead grandfather's gun or not. But once the two of those things were square in front of us, they fit together right. We weren't trying to get rich off it. We were just looking for enough money to keep up.

Lots of kids we knew either hustled drugs for their loot or pulled little stickups on the street. But drug dealers and ballplayers usually hold down opposite ends of the park, shooting looks at each other over who runs the place. That's how it was for Eddie and me with them.

The football team always had two or three posses that ripped people off. They would wave their dough around at parties and latch on to the best girls. Some of them even bought rides with their money, while Eddie and me wore out the bottoms of our good kicks walking. And whenever those dudes went out to celebrate after a big win, we were like two charity cases. Then word started getting out among the right females that Black and White were strictly welfare.

Eddie's family has more money than mine. They live two blocks down and across the street from the Ravenswood Houses, in a private house with a front porch. Eddie has a mother and a father, and they both work. Eddie gets an allowance that's only a little bigger than what I get to go to school with every week. But if Eddie ever needed twenty bucks for something, he could put his hand out and probably get it. My mother has always been tight like that. The only money coming in is from her sewing jobs, and what the state sends her every month to take care of me and my little sister.

Senior dues were $150, and the end of February was the deadline. You either paid it or missed out on everything good that went along with graduating, like the class trips to Bear Mountain and Six Flags. It took me almost three months to save that kind of money. Eddie put a lock on his wallet, too, and we were just about there.

Then around the middle of January, Nike came out

with the new Marauders. Everybody on the basketball team was buying a pair because they came in
maroon and powder blue, the same as our school colors. We were the main attraction on that squad.
There was no way we were getting caught behind
the times like that. So we spent most of our dough
on new basketball kicks. That left us with just over
a month to get the money we needed for dues. We
didn't know how we'd do it. But we made a pact that
either both of us would come up with the cash, or
we'd miss out on everything together.

Teenagers can get a job easy in some place like
McDonald's or Burger King. It's honest, but it's low-
rent, too. Kids at school and around our way already
treated us like stars. And we were going to be even
bigger one day. First in college, and then the pros. So
we decided Black and White shouldn't be serving up
fries in those stupid hats for everybody to see.
Besides, there was almost no way to juggle going to
practice every day and having a job.

That's when Eddie first snuck out the gun, thinking we could sell it. We knew a kid who paid almost
$300 for a .38 caliber just like it. But Eddie's father
knew where the gun was supposed to be and might
go looking for it one day. Eddie couldn't blame something like that on his sister. His father would have

known it was him, straight off. So we figured that we could borrow the gun anytime, then put it back. That's how we came to do stickups.

We kicked it around a lot first and knew everything we could lose. But it was only going to be a problem if we got caught. Eddie and me weren't going to be that dumb. We were just going to pull enough stickups to get the money for dues. Then we'd call it quits.

Eddie was sold on the idea before I was. "It'll be too easy," he said. "And whatever we can take, we deserve." That hit something inside, and pushed me over the line.

We knew enough not to rob other kids. They could get stupid right in the middle of it, or might have a posse of their own and come back after us. We were looking for a payday, not a war. Adults are just easier. Most of them don't want any trouble. They're scared of kids they don't know. And unless you get unlucky and try to heist an off-duty cop or corrections officer, you're usually home free. We even thought about taking the bullets out of the gun, just to play it safe. But we stressed, thinking we might have to shoot it off in the air, if there was ever any real drama.

Growing up, kids all around my way would boost

little things from stores, like candy and soda. If you got caught, the owners would beat your ass good before they'd even think about calling the cops. But I was more worried about what my mother would do to me, and how it would make her feel to know her only son was a thief. It wasn't worth it to me back then. I would rather watch everyone else getting over than turn my own mother against me.

But things were different now. I was already seventeen. I had to start pulling my own weight, until playing ball paid off in cash. It was the same for Eddie. He was my best friend, and the only one I would ever trust on something like this.

We practiced coming up on people, over and over. Eddie said we should watch how they did it on TV, because they copied things like that from the way it really goes down. So we worked on it, like any play we ever ran in a game. Then we scouted out a good-sized parking lot just off the end of Steinway Street, where people shopping might have some real cheese on them.

The lot was laid out in front of a P.C. Richards electronics store, and always deep with rows of cars. There was a big hardware store on one side of it, a movie theater on the other, and a pizza restaurant across the street. There was a sign that read, PARKING

FOR P.C. RICHARDS CUSTOMERS ONLY! But we watched, and everyone going into those other places used that lot, too. In between everything, there was a little park without a basketball hoop. It just had kiddie things in it, like a seesaw and a jungle-gym set. It was empty during the day because of the cold, and we knew it would be the same at night. So we used it as a sort of base to look things over.

Our first time out, it took almost an hour before we moved. We sat on the swings going back and forth, figuring out if we had the nerve to pull it off or not. Lots of people walked by alone, but we just watched them all. Then we started dissing each other about who was going to chicken out first. When all that ran dry, we got quiet and moved closer to the gate. We picked out a white lady carrying a shopping bag. She walked real slow. That was good for us because we wanted to keep our timing right. Eddie and me were walking even with each other, maybe twenty feet apart. And if that lady had turned around, she never would have thought we were together.

We waited until she got all the way to her car. Then Eddie came up from behind and showed her the gun. She got hysterical right away and started to cry. I took the package out of her hand so she could open her pocketbook. Her wallet was sitting right on top.

She was so scared, she couldn't pull it out. Finally, Eddie reached in and grabbed it. Then we got our asses out of there quick.

I didn't want to throw the lady's package down in the street and have somebody take a second look at us. So I just held on to it tight, and dropped my face down behind it. We weren't even a block away when she started screaming for help.

I hated the way she sounded. It was like we did something really terrible to her. After that, Eddie and me decided we'd never rob another woman.

"It's like if somebody did that to your mother," Eddie said. "How would you feel?"

I was just happy we got away with it. We were so nervous that almost a half hour went by before we looked in her wallet. There was $92 inside. So we did a little victory dance, and gave each other high fives out behind my building. We looked at the picture on her driver's license for a second, but neither one of us wanted to know her name. Then we walked a couple of blocks and threw her wallet into a big trash bin behind a supermarket, credit cards and all.

There was a brand-new Walkman in the package. Eddie said he wanted me to keep it for acting so smart and holding on to it. I scratched up the cover so it wouldn't look like it was right out of the box. Then

I gave it to my little sister, Sabrina, and told my mother I found it outside of school. Sabrina had the earphones plugged into her head for a week straight. And every time I saw her with it, I thought about what Eddie and me had done.

Two weeks after that, we robbed an old white man just before the stores closed that night. We were about to step to him when somebody passed by out of nowhere. Eddie and me just froze for five or six seconds. When I looked up again the man was already halfway into his car. I was surprised when Eddie went ahead and pulled the gun on him anyway.

Eddie's face turned mean-looking. He made the man slide over, and got into the driver's seat next to him. Then Eddie unlocked the back door, and I got in, too. He screamed at the man to empty all his pockets. I didn't see much because my eyes were glued to the side window, watching for trouble. But after the man took out his money, he had his eyes shut tight. When we bounced, Eddie grabbed the man's car keys and left them on his back bumper.

"The cops probably won't even find them back there," Eddie said.

And we walked away fast with confidence, like we were professionals now.

That job got us $129 in folding money, almost $3 in

loose change and a token to drive across the Triboro Bridge.

I remember, we stopped at the McDonald's underneath the train tracks on Broadway and each had two Quarter-Pounders with Cheese. Then we left the token on the table like a tip for anybody who wanted it.

Between our loot and what we had saved, there was enough for dues. We held on to the money over the weekend just to look at it some more. But when we went to pay that Monday, the school secretary got bent out of shape because it was March first already.

Eddie knows how to fast-talk most people good, and he didn't waste a second after the last word left her mouth. He told her I was busy celebrating Black History Month. That he thought it was a leap year, and February had the one extra day to it. She smiled at all of that nonsense and made us each out a receipt.

We were happy the way everything turned out, but were flat broke again. It all went down too easy to just walk away. And neither one of us mentioned quitting the stickup business.

Our last stickup was on the next Friday night, after basketball practice. Before we left, Coach Casey called everyone over to the bleachers and gave his usual speech for the weekend.

"Gentlemen, I know the city never sleeps, but try not to get into anything stupid over the next couple of days," Casey told the team. "Don't get into fights and don't get locked up. Do your families a favor—stay home at night and study. I want to see everybody back here on Monday the way we left."

Eddie and me would always smile at each other while Casey talked like that. Not because we didn't appreciate it, but because we knew his rap inside out. We heard him make that same speech every Friday for almost four years. But Casey was solid with us. And we knew he meant it.

On our way up to Steinway Street, Eddie asked me if I wanted to be the one to hold the gun this time. It felt good in my hand the couple of times I played around with it. But I didn't have any real practice pulling it out on somebody. Eddie had been perfect twice already. I didn't want to screw things up, so I took a pass.

It was freezing out that night. We started to shiver, waiting in the back of the parking lot, across from the park. We had our eyes locked onto everything around us, looking for somebody easy. We even passed on a man with a cane because it didn't feel right, and the wind came up strong against us.

Eddie said that holding the gun was like squeezing a piece of ice, and his fingers were going numb. So I let him have my gloves. After a while, I started blowing into my hands to keep them warm. I could see my breath coming out between my fingers, and anybody who saw us there probably thought we were smoking weed.

The man was just a shadow to me when he first came out of that hardware store. It was really dark, and he had his coat buttoned all the way up around his neck. Eddie gave me a nod, and I nodded right back. I didn't even know the man was black until we walked up to him, and Eddie told him it was a stickup.